NIGHT VIGIL

For hours I sat alone, crouched in the dark, waiting and listening, trying to ignore the corpse at my feet in its pool of blood.

Each moment I strained to hear the siren that would bring the police, as Charles had promised. And moment by moment, my fears grew. What if Charles—a stranger after all—were lying to me? What if he never returned and I was left alone, the only person at the scene of a murder—with a dead man's blood on my shoes?

Suddenly, the body slid forward, as if alive, and one hand seemed to grope towards me for help. Shaking with fear, I ran to the door and out into the night. Then I heard the footsteps behind me. . . .

1

It started like any day in Lloydsville. As usual I got up at seven because Aunt Jane hadn't approved of people lolling in bed. Self-indulgence was the first step on the road to ruin. In other words, Aunt Jane was an early riser herself.

I made tentative suggestions to Griggs, the housekeeper whom I had inherited with Aunt Jane's white elephant of a house and whom I was much too afraid of to fire. Griggs regarded me as an interloper and my inheritance as the result of some peculiarly revolting chicanery on my part. In spite of her long knowledge of Aunt Jane, she had expected a large legacy. Instead, Aunt Jane had left her the sum of one hundred dollars "in appreciation of twenty years of faithful service," and an oil painting she had done in her youth, regretted, and sensibly kept in the attic ever since.

Griggs paid no attention to orders, did as little as possible, and bullied me. But I had never been a fighter and I was willing to put up with almost anything for the sake of peace.

At that time peace seemed to me a fairly satisfying goal in life. The path of least resistance. No struggle, no dissension, no conflict. Only occasionally was I aware that I had acquired my peace at the cost of practically everything else. I was living in a kind of mental and spiritual feather bed. Soft and comfortable but passive. Dear heaven, how passive!

For the past few days I had lived practically in a

state of siege. Griggs, who knew everything about me, partly because she read any letters I left around, partly because she watched every move I made and listened to my telephone conversations, was aware that I was probably going to marry Richard Burgess. Richard, as she well knew, would make short work of her. She went around with a long face, her mouth drawn down until the corners nearly reached her chin, her first chin, at any rate, exuding resentment and a sense of ill-usage.

"You'll have your dinner at the country club," she reminded me as I held out a shopping list. Saturday night dinner at the country club was as immutable as sunrise and sunset. "And there's some of last night's chicken you could eat cold for a bite of lunch, unless you expect me to do the shopping and cook your lunch for you."

After all, there was no reason why she shouldn't, as it was what she was paid for, but after a look at her face, I took back the list and got out my small Renault to do the shopping myself; though, being a congenital coward, I tried to smother my own shame at this craven submission to a stronger will by telling myself I really wanted the ride and I'd enjoy getting out for a while.

In the supermarket, the department store, the lending library, I met my aunt's friends and heard the inevitable comments about the unseasonably harsh winter, the price of food, and the iniquities of the Administration. Then, because that evening was to be special, a landmark in a life devoid of landmarks, I bought a new dinner dress, a conservatively cut navy blue with long sleeves and a high neck. Appropriate for the occasion.

While I was dressing for dinner, Griggs stuck her head around the door—she always popped out as though she lived in a cuckoo clock—to say darkly, "Spending all your aunt's money to doll yourself up.

I owe it to her memory to tell you so. Like Sarah. That's what you'll turn out to be if you aren't careful. Like Sarah. No good."

In spite of her disapproving look I took time with my lipstick and sprayed on perfume. Then I went down to meet Richard who looked at me and raised his eyebrows.

If I had vaguely hoped for a compliment on the new dress, Richard disappointed me. "You are always prepared for minor occasions," he said.

"Minor?"

"Minor for you," he said blandly. "You are expecting me to propose to you tonight, which I have no intention of doing."

"Well—"

"Because," he went on in his deliberate way, "you are just fool enough to marry me." His voice rose to a ridiculous falsetto. "Dear old Richard, so kind and reliable. The old family friend. Standing by while Aunt Jane made life hell for me."

"That's not fair," I protested.

He ignored the interruption. "Dear Richard who provides aid and comfort as required. I owe him that much." He broke off to glare at me. It was quite a glare because he has a face like an eagle.

"There are times," he said in exasperation, "when you annoy me beyond endurance, Mary, my love. Nature endowed you with the body of a siren and the heart of a sheep. Criminal waste, that's what it is. For ten years you were a sacrificial lamb for that corrosive old woman, and let's have no mealy-mouthed hypocrisy about her. Jane Fulbright was a bully of the meanest kind, using her ill health as a weapon. Now you are free. Free. Do you know what that means? And you'd take me out of gratitude, for God's sake. A man twenty years your senior." He glared again. "The trouble with you, my girl, is that you are a born victim."

That made me laugh. "You've got it wrong, Richard. I can take care of myself. Sonia is the one who's the born victim."

"God give me strength!" His bony hand, the knuckles swollen by arthritis, gripped my shoulder, shook it. "Your cousin Sarah—oh, all right, Sonia or whatever silly name she calls herself now—is about as helpless as a barracuda. Sometimes you make me despair of your intelligence. How long do you intend to go on shielding her when she makes a fool—or worse—of herself?"

"You're prejudiced."

"Of course I am." Richard makes it difficult to argue, which is an annoying trait. "And now if you are ready, we'll go to the country club for your weekly dissipation, dinner and bridge with friends of your aunt."

"You don't make it sound like a very wild night."

"That," Richard said, "was the general idea. Much as I resent having to be just to Sonia on any count, I'll give her full marks for getting all she can out of life. You've never accepted the adventure of being yourself. Who was that French pessimist who complained, '*Mon dieu, que la vie est quotidienne.*' "

My French isn't good. I translated slowly, "How daily life is."

"Exactly. You might bear in mind that the days had better count. Make the most of them. At least, give the matter some consideration before you turn into a professional martyr, than which there is no more repellent object."

He laughed at my indignant expression and kissed me lightly on the cheek. "Tear up that list of household linen you've been making for our impending marriage and start dreaming up a glamorous wardrobe." He looked at my new dress, so carefully chosen to be a credit to him, without a trace of favor.

I hadn't made such a list but I had written Sonia to say I would probably marry Richard Burgess. I was aware of a curious sense of lightness, as though some weight had been lifted from my shoulders. Richard was aware of it, too. "Come on," he mocked me gently. "Off for your wild night."

So I walked into the beginning of the ugliness that was to culminate a week later in the wildest and most terrifying night of my life.

II

The country club is the core of social life in Lloydsville, a closed corporation that accepts no newcomers and maintains strict privacy about its activities. When it was founded, some fifty years ago, there really had been activity of a sort; but when the factories closed down, most of the young people moved away to more fertile fields and the little town was left to the well-heeled middle-aged and elderly with substantial homes, ample incomes, and a set pattern of living.

Most of these pillars of Lloydsville lived on inherited money that had been acquired before the days of the income tax. They regarded social security as the dangerous forerunner of creeping socialism, though socialism had been creeping for a hundred years without making any perceptible gains. They were dutiful if not devout churchgoers, getting much of their satisfaction from the conviction of the good example they were providing for those more in need of divine intervention than they were themselves.

A few of the newcomers, people who had settled in Lloydsville uneasily some ten to fifteen years ago and had fallen into a coma before they could get out, gave cocktail parties, which were frowned upon by the more solid citizens who did their excessive drinking in private. They had a comforting conviction that what nobody knew attained a certain respectability.

At this point I was the only person under thirty who attended the weekly dinner and bridge at the country club. Now and then I went there alone, especially since Aunt Jane's death had given me unaccustomed hours of freedom, to play tennis with the pro. Most of the members used the golf links, but the swimming pool had become little more than a decorative spot on the lawn. At no time had it been a place for reckless gaiety. There had never been any rumors of naked bathing at our swimming pool. If bathing machines were still to be found and were practicable at swimming pools, they would have made their last stand in Lloydsville.

In spite of the scandal that invariably clung to Sonia's actions, I had never blamed her for leaving Lloydsville at the first opportunity. In fact, I had never been able to blame Sonia for anything, even when the newspapers and gossip columnists made a Roman holiday of her actions. The only pity was that the first opportunity that had arisen to escape had been marriage with a man in his late fifties when she was only seventeen.

I don't need to describe Sonia to you. Every magazine has carried her picture on its cover at one time and another. And that disastrous if exciting year in Hollywood made her a household word because of her two quick divorces, and the heartthrob stories about the women whose marriages she had destroyed.

I had never believed half the stories. The pathetic death of that lovely and tragic waif Marilyn Monroe had left Hollywood without a sex symbol, so the publicity machine had made one of Sonia. People saw only that beautiful body, the elusive smile. They didn't know of the simple sweetness, the warm generosity, the naïve gullibility that made her a predestined victim. The trouble with Sonia, as I was weary of telling people, was that she believed in everyone. That was why she had made those three dreadful marriages.

At least I assumed the third marriage was as foredoomed to disaster as the others, though I had never met Jack Kenyon whom she had married a few months earlier in Las Vegas. I had learned of that marriage first when a Hollywood columnist divulged the secret wedding ceremony that had "united two of the most glamorous figures in show biz."

If I had been temporarily hurt that Sonia had not told me herself, I understood better when she wrote to explain that Jack's contract had stipulated that he remain unmarried because he was devastatingly attractive to women, and an unattached man had considerable feminine box-office appeal. The premature disclosure had caused him a lot of professional damage. Someone jealous of his success had deliberately released the story in order to get his contract revoked. Of course it hadn't been her fault but she blamed herself because it was their marriage that had caused him so much trouble.

One thing was sure; whatever people said about her, I was on Sonia's side now as I had been ever since I was ten and she, at fifteen, had fallen under Aunt Jane's displeasure. It was typical of Sonia's unlucky streak that Aunt Jane should have had one of her attacks the night Sonia slipped away without permission to go to the movies with a neighborhood boy. That was when Aunt Jane changed her will, making me her sole heir.

Even then, in spite of the five years between us, I had been the one to look after Sonia, to cover for her. Recently she had cropped off those five years for the sake of her career and she could afford to. She seemed younger than I did now. As children we had been astonishingly alike, with the same build and coloring, except that my eyes are nondescript and hers an incredible blue. By the time I was eighteen we still looked alike at first glance. The difference was that Sonia got the second glance.

I was thinking of her when Richard and I reached the country club, remembering with an upsurge of familiar resentment that on her rare visits to Lloydsville she was cold-shouldered at the club.

As usual, we stopped for a cocktail in the dimly

lighted cocktail lounge, served by the dejected-looking bartender, who put aside his crossword puzzle rather sulkily in order to mix the drinks. Gus was a typical example of Lloydsville thinking. When he reached retirement age there was a halfhearted discussion about giving him a pension. On second and more sober thought, it was decided that he would feel more self-respecting if he continued to work for his money.

The decision may have increased his self-respect but it had done nothing to improve his disposition. He cast a thick pall of gloom over the already gloomy cocktail lounge and he served drinks as though he had made them from one of the more unpleasant Borgia formulas. On the whole, I couldn't blame him for his resentment but the sight of his surly face was enough to spoil the taste of a better cocktail than he ever made.

That night there wasn't a single new face in the dining room. There wasn't a human being there whom I hadn't known all my life. We progressed slowly toward our table, partly because the encroachment of crippling arthritis made walking painful for Richard, partly because he was universally popular and everyone had something to say to him.

While we ate our way through shrimp cocktails, clear soup, and charcoal-broiled steak—the invariable Saturday night special—I noticed the speculative glances at our table. Lloydsville recognized the symptoms. I had dined five times in public with Richard and all that remained was to set the date for our wedding and determine whether we would live in his house or in the great barracks I had inherited from Aunt Jane. It amused me to realize that only Richard himself balked at the idea of my marrying a man nearly twice my age.

There were invariably six tables of bridge after the Saturday night dinner, another of the fixed institutions of Lloydsville at which Sonia had raged. Other cities had dancing but the more solid citizens of Lloydsville were too elderly for that. Anyhow, they were used to bridge. This was a solemn game, played in unbroken silence except for the bidding and scoring. Only at the end of the evening was there conversation, a somewhat acrimonious rehashing of the hands and the way in which they had been played. A lukewarm player at best, I was usually the target for most of the criticism.

Now and then Gus appeared with highballs—only one for me because I was regarded as too young to be able to handle alcohol; the rest of the time I drank ginger ale, which I loathed. Now and then the dummy left the table, strolled out onto the long porch for a breath of fresh air.

I was dummy during the last hand and I picked up my highball—my one real one—and walked out on the porch, drawing long breaths of cold air into my lungs. The evening had tired me. Perhaps it was the letdown of Richard refusing to marry me. I was tired. So tired—

Richard was shaking my shoulder. "Mary! Mary, wake up!"

I lifted my head with difficulty and Richard hauled me to my feet, holding me as I sagged against him. He must have been drinking, I thought in dull surprise. The air around him was saturated with the smell of alcohol.

"Stand up. Please try to stand up." It was the urgency in his voice, for all that it seemed a long way off, remote as a dream, that spurred me to the prodigious effort. My body didn't seem to belong to me.

"Try, Mary!" He shook me. "One foot after the other. That's it."

"Whass—wrong?" I had trouble shaping the words.

He was cursing softly, which was not like Richard. "We've got to go inside. I'm terribly sorry but there's no help for it. Mary, do you understand me?"

"Yes."

"Try to walk steadily. Right straight ahead. Can you do that?"

"Why not?" I heard myself giggling. Richard's desperate seriousness struck me as irresistibly funny. The giggles grew louder.

The door opened on lights and warmth and startled faces.

"Richard, what's wrong with Mary?"

He pushed past them, dragging me along with him. Someone said clearly, "She's drunk."

2

It was nearly noon on Sunday when I awoke with a throbbing headache and nausea. When I opened my eyes the light seemed to knife through my brain. The first heartening words I heard came from Griggs.

"Drunk and disorderly! I never thought I'd live to see the day when I would rejoice that your poor aunt had passed over. It would have broken her heart to see Mr. Burgess dragging you in, dead drunk. Couldn't even undress yourself. I had to do that."

"I couldn't have been drunk," I protested. "Not on one highball. One single, solitary highball. It's not possible." I was sorry then that I had tried to defend myself. I owed her no explanations.

"You were out like a light. You smelled like a distillery and your new dress is ruined, that's what it is, because you spilled your drink. And what's more, everyone in town knows. I've been hearing rumors all morning. I just can't stay on here any longer, Mary."

"Fine!" I said heartlessly.

She burst into tears. "That's right. Turn me out now that I've worked my fingers to the bone."

As she was about fifty pounds overweight I found myself grinning. She went out, slamming the door behind her and making my head pound.

Even public disgrace—and only heaven knew what I had been guilty of, certainly I didn't—was not an unmitigated evil if it brought with it the consolation of getting rid of Griggs. She had been like the Old Man of the Sea, an intolerable weight that there had seemed no hope of losing. Without Griggs's constant presence, her unrelenting surveillance, her perpetual disapproval, even that cumbersome house with its twelve bedrooms, two old-fashioned baths, and wide draughty corridors, would be tolerable.

I lay thinking happily that I would give Griggs five thousand dollars to make up for Aunt Jane's parsimony. It would be worth every penny. Then her words began to penetrate my befogged mind. Apparently I had made a fool—or worse—of myself the night before. Try as I would I could remember nothing about it.

An hour later, I managed to stagger out of bed, shower and dress. When I got a clear look at my face, particularly my eyes, I felt that perhaps Griggs had some justification. Holding on to the railing, I went downstairs, drank cold tomato juice, and eventually swallowed black coffee and dry toast. Griggs had gone out and I had the house to myself. An ugly house with heavy furniture, dark drapery, and big ornate lamps that gave little light.

Forty years earlier it had been the showplace of Lloydsville, the epitome of elegance in its day. Set squarely in the middle of some twenty acres of landscaped ground, with an ornamental pagoda for a summerhouse in which, to my certain knowledge, no one had sat in twenty years, it was a massive red brick, with turrets, gingerbread balconies, ironwork cropping up in unexpected places, and the last stained-glass windows in upper New York State.

The glassed-in conservatory, once famous for its flowers, now held a dejected cactus and a few dwarf orange trees on which the fruit was small and bitter. The music room, complete with concert grand piano, harp, and gilt chairs, had not been opened in my memory except for dusting. In fact, the major part of the house had been closed up by Aunt Jane and we lived in six rooms. For all her air of martyrdom, Griggs had little work to do.

Here my mother had been born and Sonia's mother. They had escaped early because they had both died after a few short years of marriage. Only Aunt Jane had remained of the three sisters to live out her life, to guard her possessions, "my things" she always called them. The only one without beauty, she had, in the long run, enjoyed the most contentment. No dreams, no aspirations, no searching. Just her things. She hadn't really possessed them; they had possessed her. Now they smothered me as the overheated club-house had smothered me the night before, and I wanted out.

That was half-past two. By six I knew I'd have to get out. Lloydsville and I had come to a parting of the ways. Griggs returned from a woman's meeting at her church to retail the gossip with gloomy satisfaction. Everyone in town knew that some woman had got drunk at the country club the night before and had indulged in what my housekeeper called "nameless orgies." Actually, with her restricted experience, I doubt if she could have named one.

By five o'clock my precarious anonymity was ended when the Town Crier, Lloydsville's gossip reporter, whom everyone disapproved of and everyone listened to, began his broadcast with the comment, "What beautiful local heiress experimented disastrously last night with the cup that cheers and sometimes inebriates?"

Aunt Jane's legacy of the big house and three hundred thousand dollars had grown in local minds to millions. Some of her dearest friends were convinced that I had used the most unscrupulous of wiles to secure that inheritance. Most of them, however, were prepared to help me dispose of it, coming up with endless suggestions for investment. Actually, apart from making a will that left everything to Sonia, I had had nothing to do with it. One thing about Aunt Jane, she would have seen that it was safely and profitably invested.

As soon as the Town Crier's broadcast was over, the telephone started ringing. No one referred to it. There wasn't the slightest reference to my behavior at the country club. Nevertheless, I had been tried in the public mind and already the verdict was in.

The first call was from Mrs. McClay, who had gone to school with Aunt Jane and had seen her weekly for fifty years. All they had had in common was a strong mutual antipathy but perhaps that had been a kind of bond between them. She told me I'd be glad to know I wouldn't have to serve on the woman's club committee after all as someone had been kind enough to substitute. The stodgy doings of middle-aged people couldn't be expected to interest me.

The doctor's wife, rather gruff and apologetic because she was innately kind, said that she and Doctor would have to cancel dinner with me this week. In quick succession my appointments were broken. Mabel had to see her dressmaker and couldn't lunch with me. The Harrises suggested I get someone else to go to the visiting symphony in their stead as they expected guests from out of town.

After that I let the telephone ring without bothering to answer.

By the time Richard arrived I was feeling suicidal. After a dismayed look at his scowl I braced myself for a moral lecture. So did Griggs who was waiting hopefully at the door to the living room.

"What has this girl had to eat today?" Richard demanded, and it was obvious that he was in a towering temper but, I realized in relief, it was not directed at me.

Griggs was as taken aback as I was. "Well, really, Mr. Burgess, she was in no condition——"

"Fix her a decent meal right away. You should have had sense enough to do that hours ago. Something nourishing but not too highly seasoned."

Griggs was a last-ditcher. "You can't expect me to know what to do for drunks."

"Drunk? That girl had knockout drops. Didn't you see her eyes? Now get busy."

She gave him a startled look, turned to stare at me, and then, to preserve her dignity, flounced out.

Richard drew up a chair beside the couch on which I had collapsed after the last telephone call. "When are you going to get rid of that poisonous woman?"

"She resigned today and I took her up on it before she knew what had happened to her."

"Good!" he said.

I grinned at him. "You needn't put on this display of cheer for my benefit. I heard the Town Crier."

"I'd like to break his neck. Of all the filthy, malicious, uncalled-for comments, that was his worst yet."

"It doesn't really make any difference, does it? Everyone at the club must know. Richard, how badly did I behave and how could it have happened? I had only one highball. Honestly, I did."

Belatedly I took in what he had said. "Was that true? About the knockout drops?"

"You were doped to the hilt. I knew that last night after I got you home and had a good look at you. Before that I had thought—well, you were at loose ends and all that because I wasn't going to let you throw yourself away on me. A kind of celebration."

"Richard!"

He brushed aside my protest. It would, he assured me, have been a perfectly natural reaction. Not the drinking, perhaps, but the celebration. He'd been a bit worried, however, when Gus told him I'd been drinking highballs all evening.

"Richard! That's not true."

It was only, he said, after he had got me home and had a close look at me that he realized the trouble wasn't an excess of alcohol but drugs of some kind.

"I should have called your physician right then but you didn't seem to be in any danger and there would have to be an investigation, some sort of publicity probably. I knew you would hate that. On the other hand, I couldn't simply let the thing go. So this morning I went to Gus's rooming house. He'd cleared out. Not a trace of him except for a typed letter in the wastebasket saying he'd find enclosed five hundred dollars in cash, and that the job must be done on Saturday night."

"Gus," I said blankly. "Gus did that to me. But why, Richard?"

"Obviously for five hundred dollars."

"But who on earth would—"

"I'll never rest until I lay my hands on Gus Futrell," Richard assured me. "And he's going to talk."

Griggs set up a card table beside the couch, covered it with Aunt Jane's lace tablecloth and put on the best silver and crystal. She didn't glance at me but she was nervously aware of Richard who watched her in sardonic silence.

She brought in bowls of her famous clam soup, flaky muffins, and a golden omelet crisped at the edges.

When she had cleared away that perfectly prepared light supper and was busy in the kitchen—she always worked noisily as though to assure people that she was being brutally exploited—Richard lighted his pipe and leaned back in his chair. I found him watching me, an odd expression on his face.

"It's such a queer thing to have happened," I said miserably. "I can't understand it. Even for the money, supposing that was behind it, why would Gus dope me, why would he lie about those drinks?"

"He's hated the lot of us since they decided not to give him a pension."

"But why me?"

"You're asking the wrong question. It's not 'why

me,' but who put Gus up to it and gave him the money for the job?"

"I can't say that question is much easier to answer."

"Either," Richard said tartly, "you aren't thinking or you don't want to think. This wasn't merely a matter of making you appear drunk. The whole town had to know about it. It was deliberately contrived, you know. No member of the country club would have given the Town Crier that story or let it leak out the way it did. Much as they relish their scandals they keep them for private delectation."

"Oh." All of a sudden I realized that it was true. Few of the older people trusted me completely because of my ominous resemblance to Sonia; a number of them resented my inheriting Aunt Jane's money; not one of them was likely to believe any explanations I might be able to offer for last night's affair or to let me forget it. But not a single one of them would have let the story go beyond the club itself.

Richard looked at me curiously. "That hadn't occurred to you?"

I shook my head numbly. "I don't seem to be able to think straight about anything that has happened."

"There's only one straight way to think about it. The whole incident was deliberately staged. Someone is out to make Lloydsville too hot for you and, if I'm not mistaken this is only the beginning."

The idea was preposterous but I couldn't think of a more plausible explanation. I turned his question back on him.

"Why, Richard?"

The telephone rang and, because of Richard's fortifying presence, I dared to answer. It was Sonia's voice in a rush of words, warm and sweet and loving as usual.

"Mary darling, I've just had the most wonderful idea! I've been listening to weather reports. It must be horrible up there. Darling Mary, come to us.

Please, please, come to us. Leave that beastly cold and come to Florida where it's all sunshine and palm trees. Oh, Mary, please come. Now. Right away. This minute. And don't bother to dig out last summer's clothes. They wouldn't be suitable here. You can get anything you need after you arrive, and a much better choice for the season. Just pack an overnight bag and come on."

Before she rang off she had persuaded me to leave the next day. I was just to turn the key in the door and go. Let Griggs pick up after me. It wouldn't hurt her to do some work for a change. But I wasn't used to making thousand-mile drives, she warned me. I was to promise to call her every single day so she wouldn't worry.

When I turned to face Richard, I was weak with relief. Instead of the future holding misery and embarrassment, it was opening up with exciting prospects: Florida and sunshine and palm trees; Sonia with her loyalty and affection; doors to adventure standing wide open.

"Bless Sonia!" I said fervently. "She never fails. I'll give Griggs a nice check to make up for Aunt Jane's meanness—I had intended to do that, anyhow—and leave her to close the house. I don't care much if I never open it again. Aside from you, Richard, there's no one here who matters to me. Not one."

Richard was silent. After a long time he said with a hesitation that was unlike him, "You know that proposal I refused to make last night, like the arrogant ass I am? Consider it made, will you, Mary?"

Seeing my profound surprise, something like dismay I could not entirely conquer, he added quickly, "Keep it in mind. Just in case."

He did not let me answer. He stood looking down at me, his face thoughtful and troubled. With a warmth he had never before permitted himself, he bent to kiss me. And then he was gone.

3

There were snowstorms and icy roads until I was south of Richmond. Once I was holed up for eight hours in my freezing car until I could be dug out of a snowdrift, along with a dozen other stalled passenger cars and trucks, an operation that took endless hours. After that I lay for twenty-four hours in a motel bed with a cold and fever.

The first half of the trip was a looking back at Lloydsville and Aunt Jane, at the wasted years of my girlhood, at the unswerving and understated devotion of Richard, at that ugly and inexplicable affair at the country club. No matter in what light I regarded it, the whole business was senseless.

Gus had understandably felt bitter about his treatment; he was a pushover for anyone who wanted to capitalize on his grievances. But who had paid him that five hundred dollars? Who had known of the Town Crier and which pool would set up ripples of gossip? What had been the purpose of that whole ugly business? "To make Lloydsville too hot for you," Richard had said. It was strange to know that someone hated me that much.

Below Richmond I put away the confusing past and began to look ahead. The days grew warmer. Even the long bleak stretches of North and South Carolina were interesting to me because I had traveled so little.

Savannah, with Spanish moss dripping from trees, was a foretaste of the South. And then there was

Florida, deep-blue skies and palm trees, women in summer dresses and men in shorts and loud sport shirts. An atmosphere of perpetual holiday to which I responded with an exhilaration and delight that would have alarmed Aunt Jane's friends to whom I had always appeared to be a sedate kind of Mother's Little Helper but imperiled by Sonia's horrible example. In Lloydsville she was still called by her maiden name, Sarah Collins, as though by ignoring her professional name, they could ignore her activities.

I had always been the kind of person who follows the beaten track, who filled my days with routine, who took the same familiar roads and streets when I did my shopping. But now, for the first time in my life, I was intoxicated with a sense of freedom. Florida had gone to my head. Impatiently I pushed aside the road map and took secondary winding roads that would lead to the beach. I felt carefree and irresponsible and I acted that way. But Sonia, to whom I reported faithfully every day, was greatly amused and approved heartily of my unorthodox behavior.

It was six days before I reached the small Florida beach resort on the Gulf where Sonia was staying with her third husband, Jack Kenyon. I parked in front of the shabby three-story hotel, with its row of chairs on the veranda and a rocking-chair brigade watching the people who strolled—so slowly it seemed to my northern eyes—along the sidewalk.

The hotel was my first inkling that things were not going well with Sonia. The Colony and "21," the luxury spots of Hollywood and Las Vegas, New York, and Paris, had been her natural milieu. She had been surrounded by a horde of people: her hairdresser, maid, secretary, public-relations man, agent. Locusts I had regarded them; the sycophants who batten on a prosperous celebrity.

Actually, I realized now, her professional career had been both spasmodic and brief. There had, after all, been only one year in Hollywood when she had shot to fame and stardom like a rocket and had gone down like a falling star because of the implacable hostility she aroused in women who regarded her as their natural enemy. After that debacle she had made television and guest appearances and sung in night clubs, culminating in a six-week engagement at Las Vegas, where she had met Jack Kenyon. She couldn't act but she had a sweet, husky voice, small but adequate with a mike; she was beautiful, and she had the essential quality for success—vitality that was like electricity in the air. People might dislike Sonia; they couldn't ignore her.

I was aware of the incongruity of my drab, heavy clothes in this setting of brilliant colors; shaking out wrinkles, I made hasty repairs on my neglected face. For the first time I regretted following Sonia's advice and bringing only a weekend bag. It would be nice to make my first appearance in something cool and fresh and attractive.

The bright light made me squint and I shoved on dark glasses, comforting myself that no one was likely to notice the resemblance between us. I wouldn't disgrace Sonia.

The lobby of the little hotel was not overclean. There were a few worn chairs and a counter with pigeonholes behind it into which a bored-looking young-old man in shirt sleeves was lazily tossing letters. He turned around as I approached the counter.

"Miss Sonia Colette?"

His expression quickened with interest as I mentioned Sonia's professional name. "Second floor. Room 218. Take the stairs. The elevator's broke." As I turned away he said hopefully, "Ma'am, you mind taking up their mail? We're short of help here."

A maid who was pushing a cart of dirty linen along the second floor said in a soft voice, "Room 218? Yes, ma'am, around the corner on your left."

There were raised voices behind the closed door of Room 218. A man was saying irritably, "For God's sake, calm down. There's nothing to get in such a flap about."

"It's all happening too fast. Everything at once. Suppose they meet?"

"They won't. Anyhow, we can't play it the way we rehearsed it. We need a new script. But quick."

"Any slip now——" Sonia began.

"Oh, stop bellyaching! Whose idea was this in the first place? Who had it all worked out, cue by cue, scene by scene?"

"I know, but if anything goes wrong—if only she would come! She should be here by now."

It dawned on me that she was worried because I was late. I knocked at the door.

"Sonia," I called, "it's Mary."

There was a little cry, then high heels tapped rapidly over the floor and the door was flung open. Sonia threw her arms around me and I was engulfed in the familiar aura of bath powder and perfume and her own special warmth and affection.

"Mary darling! Come in." Eager hands dragged me inside the room. "This is Jack. You've simply got to like each other because I love you both so much."

"So you are Sonia's little cousin." Jack Kenyon stood staring at me with mingled surprise and amusement, which I couldn't misunderstand. He was seeing both the resemblance and the differences between us.

I disliked him on sight. He was too good-looking. His handshake was too lingering. His expression was too admiring. Or rather, it demanded admiration. I realized at once that I had seen him before. One night I had switched on a television program and caught the last half of a show from Las Vegas. Jack had been singing one of those repellent self-pitying ballads about the girl he'd never forget, wandering from table to table, carrying a mike, smiling into the eyes of flattered older women, touching their hands, trailing his fingers along their arms, giving them a great big thrill.

He was a little under average height with black hair and eyes. He had a boyish figure, a boyish smile, and he sang boyish songs. In the merciless light of midday I saw that he wasn't young. He must be in his early forties; already the skin under his jaw had become slack.

"Well?" Sonia demanded eagerly.

Jack smiled his boyish smile. "I like her."

"Of course you do. What have I been telling you? Sit down, Mary." She glanced around helplessly, brushed some clothes off a chair onto the unmade bed. Then, for a long moment, we looked at each other, searching, as people must through the changes of the years, for the familiar image we had kept or, more likely, created for ourselves out of our own personal needs.

Sonia spoke first, with that odd, enigmatic smile the photographers so loved. "Darling Mary, you are just the same. Exactly the same. I told Jack you would be."

She began to drift around the room, picking things up and putting them down. Never an orderly person, she had of recent years been surrounded by helping hands. Now she seemed to be engulfed in chaos.

"You look wonderful for a girl who has just had flu. I told you Florida would be good for you."

"Except for the madness with which it has afflicted me."

"It gets you out of yourself," Jack said.

"Well, it got me out, anyhow," I admitted, and we all laughed.

The look Jack gave me was shrewdly appraising, taking in the dark, dowdy clothes, the mussed hair that I'd pulled back negligently into a knot, the sunglasses. "Must have surprised the room clerk when you asked for your cousin."

"I didn't claim Sonia as my cousin!" My voice was edged with anger.

Jack flashed his boyish smile. "I didn't mean what

you thought I did. You're quite a dish, Mary." This, he obviously felt, was an accolade.

Sonia, who knows me rather well, said hastily, "Jack, why don't you finish your errands now while Mary and I catch up with the gossip about the old home town?"

He looked at her and, apparently reading the urgent message in her eyes, said, "Fine. You two girls go ahead and talk. I have things to attend to, anyhow. See you later." He turned back from the door. "Damn, I forgot to cash a check and it's Saturday. Give me fifty, will you, sweetie?"

"Oh, Jack, I counted on you cashing a check. I haven't more than three or four dollars."

"I can let you have some," I said. "I still have about a hundred dollars. Fortunately, there was a month's housekeeping money, for I left so early Monday morning I couldn't get any travelers' checks."

"Swell." Jack took my billfold out of my hand and removed the bills. All of them. "Dependable Mary. That's what Sonia calls you."

No girl of twenty-four wants to be characterized as dependable. It sounds like some long-lasting floor wax.

"Give the little cousin my IOU." Jack saluted me with a boyish wave, which I recognized from Las Vegas as his signature, and went out.

When the door had closed on him, Sonia said, "Jack is simply adorable. You're going to love him. Every woman does. And he's got what it takes. All he needs are a few decent breaks." She looked at the letters I was still clutching. "What are they?"

"I forgot. The clerk asked me to bring up your mail."

She almost snatched the letters from me, riffled through the envelopes, dropped them on the carpet. "Bills! Wouldn't you know?"

The telephone rang and she sprawled across the bed to answer it. For the first time I had an oppor-

tunity to study her unobserved, to try to analyze the
change that had so startled me. The beautiful body
was still the same, the blonde hair the same, the
famous smile the same. She was as lovely as ever but
she was almost vibrating with tension and there were
dark smudges under the big blue eyes. My heart sank
as I recognized the familiar symptoms. Sonia was in
trouble again.

"Of course," she said after listening for some time,
"it's a wonderful break and you were marvelous to
arrange it. Jack's out but I'll tell him as soon as he
comes in. He'll be thrilled. The only hitch . . . oh, it's
just that my cousin came to visit me. Got here a few
minutes ago. . . . Oh, great. I know she'd love it. Be
seeing you."

She turned to look at me. "Talk about lucky
breaks! Only two more shows to do here tonight and
then we are going on to Arizona. Three weeks in a
smart club. Better than this crummy joint."

I had taken off my coat and hat, found a place for
them at the end of the unmade bed. Sonia flung off
her negligee and squeezed into a girdle.

"I haven't gained an ounce, but what a brutal struggle it is. How on earth do you keep your figure?"

"An upright life and no temptations," I said dryly.

She looked at me quickly and then laughed. "We'll
cure you of that." She dropped soiled clothes on the
floor and set to work on her face, talking rapidly,
telling me about Jack, about the new engagement
that had just cropped up, about the one that was to
terminate that night. This date in Florida had been
just a filler, but a friend of Jack's had arranged it and
he hadn't liked to hurt his feelings by refusing.

"I'm looking forward to seeing you both perform,"
I said.

"Oh, darling!" For a moment Sonia was intent
while she concentrated on doing her lips, then she
turned around to face me. "I am sick about it. Just
sick. But the thing is that this is the only hotel—and

it's filled up. Some damned convention. Didn't you notice those hags on the porch? Wives. Came down to keep an eye on their men and make sure they don't stray. They need a little supervision, if you ask me. I don't know which is worse: the dirty old men staring or their frumpy wives glaring. Well, if they don't try to keep themselves up, they don't get any sympathy from me."

Wives, it occurred to me, had never got much sympathy from Sonia. She had always modeled herself on the man with whom she was currently in love. This new strain of vulgarity did nothing to increase my liking for Jack Kenyon. It occurred to me that I had been too precipitate in accepting the invitation, that it would be difficult to bridge the gap between us. At least this unexpected engagement that had altered their plans could alter my own without embarrassment.

"So," she went on, stopping to pick up her discarded negligee, "we'll just have to manage the best we can tonight. Tomorrow we'll fix things. Jack will work it out." She lifted a sleeveless dress carefully over her hair, pulled it down over her hips.

"There's bound to be a motel or something," I suggested.

"Not where you could possibly stay." She was firm about that. "And no beachcombing in a place like this. It's too dangerous. But Jack has an idea. Did I tell you about his trailer? I must have written you about it; we love it so."

"Trailer?" I repeated stupidly. The idea of Sonia in a trailer was beyond me.

"He got it at Las Vegas, won it in some game. Then he kept it as a gag and we've come to adore it. Sometimes I think it is the only real life, simple and friendly. But of course, it's not practical when we are working; it spoils the sophisticated image our manager likes to create of us. Anyhow, if you wouldn't mind spending the night there—it's really a little house on wheels, you know, cosy and comfortable."

I did mind. But before I could raise any objection she sheered away to casual questions about Lloydsville, about Aunt Jane's death and the old house she had left me.

"I suppose you'll sell it," she said. "It's big enough for a hotel. You ought to get at least fifty thousand, with those beautiful grounds, especially the way the place is landscaped."

"You don't realize how it has run down; the grounds have gone to seed. Aunt Jane didn't bother with gardens the last couple of years. And then, toward the end, she never left the house. She didn't seem to care any more."

"But there always used to be people wanting to buy the place. Remember that queer woman who wanted to turn it into some sort of art center?"

"I haven't made any plans. After all, she died only three months ago. So far I've just been drifting." Just putting in time, or rather letting it slip through my fingers like sand through an hourglass, never to be recovered.

"But you can do anything you like now," Sonia pointed out. "With all that money."

What I didn't want was to return to Lloydsville but something kept me from telling Sonia about that sordid business at the country club. I had an uncomfortable feeling that she would think it was funny.

The shabbiness of that hotel room, the chaos that indicated she no longer was surrounded by helping hands, was so obvious that there was no sense in pretending I wasn't aware of it.

"If you need it, I'd like to share," I said. "That would be only fair."

"You're a love, Mary, but it wouldn't make sense to divide it. There's not enough to keep more than one in comfort. Anyhow, I can just imagine Richard Burgess agreeing to that. He's never liked me. Acted as though he thought I was a tramp."

"Oh, no, Sonia."

She flashed me a smile. "Darling Mary, you're so innocent. So unsuspecting. I've always believed Richard was the one who persuaded Aunt Jane to disinherit me in the first place."

"That's silly. No one ever persuaded her to do anything. Anyhow, why would he do a thing like that?"

"Well, my trusting love, he had his eye on you even then."

I laughed because it was too idiotic to make me angry. "You goop! I was only ten when she made that will."

"And there are no unattached males in Lloydsville. Well, maybe I'm unfair. I guess I'm prejudiced because Richard was always so beastly to me. Let's forget it. When are you two going to be married?"

I don't know what made me answer as I did, perhaps some obscure idea of attesting to my unshaken faith in Richard. "We haven't set the date yet."

"I hope he didn't mind too much about my bringing you down here."

I jumped at the opening she had given me. "He thought it was a grand idea, but, of course, that was while you planned to stay in Florida; it was before you got this new job in Arizona."

"Oh, that's all right. My agent said we could bring you along to Arizona. You'll love it. You know the gag: pack up your sinuses and take them to Arizona."

"Perhaps I'll do that another time. I don't care much for desert scenery. You go to Arizona and I'll drive back to New York. Maybe I'll spend a few days seeing plays before I go home."

As I said, Sonia knows me rather well. From my voice she grasped that I had made up my mind. She lighted a cigarette, drew on it once, and then deliberately snapped it in two.

"Mary, there's something I want to—well, I was wondering—"

Alerted by the familiar note of appeal in her voice, I asked, "What's wrong? Are you in a jam?"

"Not exactly, only—look, Mary, will you promise to do something for me?"

"If I can."

"Thank God for you, darling. You've never broken a promise in your life."

"I've never made a promise blindly," I reminded her. "I'd have to know what I was pledging myself to do."

"It's nothing, really. Just to give someone a letter."

"That sounds simple enough."

Her hand gripped mine, her long nails biting into my flesh. I was dismayed to discover how cold she was. Then I saw the stark terror looking out of her eyes. In a moment she had relaxed; she was smiling.

"What have you got yourself into, Sonia?"

The smile faded. "A mess," she said bluntly. "A terrible mess. The worst thing that has ever happened to me."

Knowing her tendency to dramatize herself, I said skeptically, "Is it really that bad?"

"It's really that bad. I did a crazy thing. I trusted someone. I thought he was all right, just sort of pitiful, and I turned over just about everything I have in the world to him."

"Sonia, you idiot! Won't you ever grow up?"

Her face crumpled like a hurt child's. "I know. And it turns out that he is really awful. And he wants more. And—you can't let me down, Mary."

"Have I ever?"

With that amazing resilience of hers, her face smoothed out and her eyes were clear and laughing again. She got up to paw through a dresser and brought me a sealed, unaddressed envelope.

"Where do I take this?" I asked, resigned.

"He'll come to the trailer for it tonight."

I didn't want to spend the night in a trailer but it began to look as though I would have to. "You aren't fool enough to be paying blackmail, are you?"

She looked at her watch rather pointedly. "With two shows to do tonight, we'll have to rehearse this afternoon. Do you think you could be ready to leave soon?"

"Right away. But I wish now I'd brought some summer clothes."

We were still the same size, she said, and there must be something of hers I could wear so that I'd be cool and more comfortable. And, of course, I'd want a swimsuit. She hunted around and then brought out a bathing bag. "Everything is in there. The suit will fit you." Over my protests she produced a dress, a backless linen sheath that revealed as much as it concealed, but at least it was cool.

She studied me for a moment and then pushed me into a chair before the mirror. "Let me do something to your hair, for heaven's sake." With nimble fingers she brushed and combed and teased and pinned until my hairdo was a reasonable facsimile of hers.

She did my lips in a wide brilliant curve, darkened my brows, and applied blue eye-shadow to my lids. There was a crunching sound and she said, "Damn, I've stepped on your dark glasses. Never mind, you can take mine." She gave me a pair that had odd triangular-shaped rims with some glittering stuff on them and stood back to survey her handiwork. There was triumph in her voice.

"There, that's the way you ought to look."

I stared at my reflection in surprise. I didn't look like Mary Quarles. I looked like Sonia Colette.

4

There wouldn't, Sonia assured me, be any difficulty in finding the trailer park. It was only five miles away, right on the beach and, except for the manager's cottage and some unoccupied house trailers, there wasn't a thing. Out of the world. It was heaven. Like being on a desert island.

The place had nearly been destroyed in a hurricane in the fall and the manager hadn't rebuilt it yet, though, with the rugged winter in the north, she expected people to come any day. Jack's was the only Scotty. In fact, it was the only travel trailer, so I couldn't miss it.

When I got into my little Renault, which I had stupidly parked in the sun, I was grateful for Sonia's thin dress. The wheel was scorching to the touch. I followed directions, driving through flat, uninteresting country, most of it mangrove swamp and clumps of palmetto. Now and then a white heron flashed against the dark jungle; now and then I slowed down to look at the walking trees that stepped out delicately into the water.

Everywhere there were real-estate signs, advertising manors and estates, though what they were really selling was uncleared and undrained swampland on vast patches of bleak sand, making a determined and fiercely competitive bid for the new wealth coming their way in the shape of Social Security.

And then there was the sparkling sea, white sands, gulls soaring and dipping, a breeze that lifted my hair and my spirits. As a rule I don't care much for the ocean. I'm a mountain and tree lover myself, the great quiet, enduring things. The unending restlessness of the ocean brings me no peace.

But here, even the water was sleepy, with sailboats drifting over it, skimming and dipping; absurd pelicans rising with a great flapping of wings and dropping with a flat splash as they caught sight of some unlucky fish. Fishermen leaned over the countless bridges with dangling lines in their hands and the peaceful air of men who have all the time in the world. All the time that is left.

Here and there people walked bent over along the shore, which struck me as a singularly uncomfortable form of locomotion until I realized they were shelling. This part of Florida, I recalled, was one of the world's great shelling areas.

When I saw the trailer-park sign I braked for a turn, almost striking a bicycle that had been propped against the signpost. A Seminole who was raking the ground looked up for a moment but without curiosity. He did not speak and I realized that he did not expect me to speak either, that he assumed I looked on him as an inseparable part of the landscape.

"Beautiful day, isn't it?" I called.

He turned in surprise, smiled at me. "Sure is." He took a look at my untanned skin. "Always like this in Florida," he said.

"You and the Chamber of Commerce." I laughed and he laughed, too.

There was a hibiscus hedge; Chinese-red bougainvillaea grew over the roof of a small weather-beaten cottage, making a breathless display of color. Somewhere nearby, a mockingbird was singing its heart out, going through its whole repertoire. Now and then, as though unbearably excited by its own music, it leaped in the air and turned completely around.

Perhaps, after all, I wouldn't find the night as strange and unpleasant as I had expected. There were unforeseen compensations. But one night, I had already determined, was to be my last. Tomorrow I would send myself a telegram and leave, if not for Lloydsville, then for somewhere else. Anywhere else.

Because something was wrong. The envelope I was carrying in my handbag indicated that. This time Sonia had got herself into real trouble. I had seen her in many moods—from stormy tears to frantic despair —but never with stark terror showing in her eyes.

For the first time I could understand Richard's exasperation when I responded to Sonia's appeals for help. I knew as well as I knew anything that I ought to get away before I became involved. But I had never in my life failed Sonia and I couldn't do it now. Nevertheless, I told myself that this was to be the last time. The very last. Because Sonia had changed in ways I didn't like; she had grown a little vulgar and strident; she had become like Jack Kenyon and I wouldn't have trusted him an inch.

I wished now that I hadn't let him take all my available cash. Of course, on Monday I could arrange for a bank draft, but I'd feel more comfortable with some money in my purse for emergencies.

I got out of the Renault, picked up Sonia's bathing bag, which I had tossed on the back seat, and locked the door. As I was about to remove my key a woman came out of the cottage, a middle-aged woman with run-down shoes, slip hanging below her dress, hair chopped off as though she had done it herself or had it done at a pet shop.

"Miss Quarles," she called and waved her hand.

I looked at her in surprise, wondering how she knew my name. She went inside her cottage and then came back across the park to the Renault with an unwrapped bottle of bourbon, which she held out to me.

"Mr. Kenyon left it. Said to enjoy yourself."

"When did he leave this?" I asked in surprise.

"Just a few minutes ago. He came to open up your

trailer so's it would be nice and cool. Put in some
groceries in case you didn't feel like going out. He's a
sweet guy. A heart as big as the world. You don't
often find that in such a handsome fellow. He sure
was surprised to see I'd got in some new people today. Said I'd have the place booming in another
week. Always one for a pleasant word. No moods
with him. No, siree. No tantrums or meanness there."

As I made no comment, her loose mouth worked
in a smile, the smile of a woman who has seen and
experienced a great deal of evil. "Well, have fun."

I was sorely tempted to drive straight on; all that
restrained me was Sonia's letter, which I had promised to deliver to the man who was to call at the
trailer for it. What puzzled me was why Jack, instead
of serving as my guide, had come on ahead. I wondered, a trifle uneasily, if he knew or suspected the
jam that Sonia was in. I felt sure that she didn't want
him to know, that she was afraid to have him know.

I wondered, too, how he had managed to pass me
on that narrow road from town without my seeing
him. There hadn't been half a dozen cars on the
whole trip. Of course I had been looking at the ocean.
I might easily have missed him. But he could hardly
have missed me, knowing that I was coming this way.
He would instinctively have been on the lookout.
He'd have hailed me. Wouldn't he?

II

Jack's little trailer was surprisingly cool. An awning,
open windows, and a small electric fan, as well as the
fresh breezes from the Gulf, kept the temperature
pleasant. In the icebox and in the cabinet above it I
found not only plenty of food but the kind of food I
like best. This thoughtfulness was so like Sonia that
for a moment all my tenderness came flooding back.

But my intention did not waver. I was going on,
somewhere, anywhere. Because I had a conviction,

deep if irrational, that I was being maneuvered, and I didn't like it at all.

I didn't like that sealed envelope, which I was to turn over to an unknown man. I didn't like the expression on the manager's face when she had handed me the bottle of bourbon. I didn't like the fact that Jack had given it to her rather than leaving it in the trailer. I didn't like the way the woman had said, "Have fun."

For a little while I sat in the trailer. From one side I could see the park itself, asleep under the southern sun. There were three large house trailers and three smaller travel trailers, one of them Jack's little Scotty. Beyond lay the wreckage of a house trailer, an uprooted palm, and the white bones of mangrove killed by the fury of last fall's hurricane.

Everywhere there were palm trees, some of them tall and stately, some of them with lovely slanting lines from having leaned against the wind, some of them stubby, with fronds hanging, like a deserted house with the wallpaper peeling off. There's nothing so dismal as a really tacky palm tree.

From the other window of the trailer I could see the beach with its soft white sand and sparkling water. This was, unbelievably, February. Only a few days earlier I had been dug out of snowdrifts, had huddled for hours in an unheated car. The longer I looked at the water the more it called me. Tomorrow I would leave the ocean behind me but today I was going to swim and lie on that incredibly soft white sand.

Before changing to Sonia's suit I might as well unpack my weekend bag. That was when I discovered that the car key, which I had left in the lock when the manager called me, was gone. I hunted through my handbag, went back to look on the table in the trailer, returned to search the sand around the Renault. Then, rather blankly, I started back to the trailer and remembered the spare in my Hide-a-Key box under the hood of the motor. That was gone, too.

I walked across the park to the office. The manager must have been watching my search because she opened the door before I could knock. With the charm that had distinguished her from the beginning she snapped, "What's wrong now?"

"I've lost my car key."

"Probably dropped it in the sand."

"I looked. Anyhow, my extra key is gone, too."

"They'll turn up if you look real good. Maybe you just got absent-minded."

"Not so absent-minded that I took the spare key out of that Hide-a-Key box and mislaid it."

"No one took your keys, if that's what you are suggesting." She had small, watery eyes screwed up as though she were perpetually weeping. "Nice people I get here. Never any trouble. Two new renters for my house trailers and those two travel trailers come in today. Nice people," she repeated. "And they've all got bigger cars than that little foreign job of yours. What would they want with it?"

I didn't know, but I still didn't believe two keys could disappear accidentally. There was no point in discussing it further with the manager who had disliked me at first sight as, indeed, I had disliked her.

Again I marveled at Sonia's blind spot about people. To her this trailer park was a retreat into a kind of unspoiled paradise. To me, particularly with that woman's eyes on me, that loose mouth working, it seemed more like a hideout.

Back in the trailer I made a new search for the keys. I could have lost one, though it was unlikely. But two? I simply didn't believe it. And unless I could find them I was completely and beautifully stuck.

At length I gave up and changed into Sonia's swimsuit. At first I was dismayed. It was as close to being a bikini as made no difference. I could imagine Griggs's horror when she saw it. Perhaps that was why

I decided to wear it, my gesture of defiance to Lloyds-ville, even though it was made at a safe distance.

I picked up Sonia's cap, terry-cloth robe, and dark glasses. Except for some sea gulls, and a small boy who was making friends with a mongrel dog, I had the beach to myself. After half an hour in the water I came out to lie face down on the soft white sand, the sun hot and healing on my skin. I didn't think of anything. I heard the rhythmic beat of the water lapping on the beach, and then nothing at all.

I must have slept for a long time. What roused me was the shrill sound of sea gulls as they fluttered wildly over my head. Although the sun was no longer hot, my skin was burning. Stupidly enough, I hadn't realized that February sun could blister.

I saw long legs, looked up, startled, into a pair of oddly colorless eyes that looked back into mine with a kind of surprise. He was in his middle thirties, with sandy hair, a face made up of hard planes, a thin mouth like a trap, and a short, stubborn jaw. A few freckles across his nose made him seem almost human. Almost. He wore only shorts and on his neck there was an ugly, jagged scar. He took a long cool look at me in my scanty suit and I scrambled to my feet.

"You've got a bad burn. The Florida sun is dangerous. You should know better."

"Did you come out here to tell me that?"

"Well, not altogether." Again those colorless eyes looked me over and I practically dived for the beach robe, slipped into it and shoved the dark glasses into my pocket.

"Do you have any sunburn lotion?" He seemed to be impervious to snubs.

"No."

"I'll bring you some. Otherwise you won't sleep tonight. That burn is going to hurt. What you need is a little drink."

"Miss Quarles has a little drink," the manager said nastily from nearby, and after a sharp look at both of us she turned away.

The man with the colorless eyes still stood beside me. "Quite a sight," he said, and then I really noticed the sea gulls. There seemed to be hundreds of them swirling around. The manager was throwing out pieces of bread, and a small crowd had gathered to watch. The gulls soared and dipped, hovering overhead, wings fluttering, making shrill cries. When one of them snatched a piece of bread, the others pursued him, trying to take it away instead of getting one of their own, just like human beings.

When the manager had disposed of the last of the bread she said, "Now, folks, I know how it is. You people will feel more at home if you know each other."

She indicated a young couple, the girl with a laughing face, the young man tanned and muscular, the parents of the small boy. "These here are the Millers from Detroit."

A heavy-set middle-aged man with small eyes and one of those dark beards that have to be shaved twice a day, and a woman wearing too-short shorts and a tight halter over a plump body, she introduced as the Browns from Toronto.

"We are refugees from the cold," Mrs. Brown said vivaciously. "I just love hot weather but not too hot, if you know what I mean. And not too primitive either. I'm a city girl. Beaches are one thing; jungle's another."

This, apparently, was a grievance addressed to her husband rather than to us. He chuckled.

"I took Mabel on one of those jungle tours. She didn't like it."

"Like it! There were rattlers on the ground and moccasins in that filthy black water and an alligator half-buried in mud, looking at me with its little red eyes. It was horrible. Once when our boat stopped, I like to have died. There was no walking back from that place. I can tell you, never again, Glenn! And I mean never."

Her husband grunted, "Yeah, yeah," wearily as though they had had this out before, looked me over as though I were on an auction block, fingering his heavy jowls. Then he winked at me. His wife saw him, took his arm, and turned abruptly toward the biggest of the house trailers. As might be expected, the manager saw that roving eye, too. The look she gave me made me gather the robe closely around me, feeling naked.

An elderly pair were introduced as the Batesons from Indiana, the sandy-haired man was Mr. MacIntosh from California, and "that girl"—I realized by the gracious words she meant me—was Miss Quarles.

Mrs. Bateson gave me a friendly smile. "Where you from?"

"Upper New York State."

"We've got that new travel trailer. This is just like the pitchers in the travel ads, isn't it: the beach and the gulls, sunset with palm trees silhouetted against it, and you for the pretty girl in the ads." She smiled without malice. "Mrs. Brown wouldn't quite fit, would she, though she tries hard. Pore thing, trying to hold a man who don't want to settle down. And Mrs. Thomson wouldn't fit, either."

"Mrs. Thomson?"

The bright, observant old eyes looked at me in surprise. "The manager. Said you'd been here two, three days, so I thought you'd know her name."

Before I could assure her that I wouldn't be caught dead here for even one day, she nodded toward a frail elderly man. "That's Bateson. Just retired and he still don't hardly know what to do with hisself. I told him we'd been in one spot too long and it was time we tried something new. But he don't seem to have the taste for it. Drifting, he says. But he'll like it well enough when he can play shuffleboard with other retired men and they can talk about where they come from and all that. Maybe he can get interested in fishing or shelling. Thing is, we put our savings into that trailer, so I say he's got to learn to like it."

She sounded rather defiant but the eyes that watched her husband were, I thought, anxious. Her voice dropped. "He don't know it but he has a heart condition. Real bad. Any shock could be fatal to him. The doctor wants him to live in the sun and take things easy."

She dived into a capacious handbag. "Got some pitchers of the children and grandchildren. Don't seem possible they can grow up so fast." She fished them out, as unattractive a lot as I'd encountered for a long time, so far as I could make out in the uncertain light. She gave me a friendly smile. "You better do something about that sunburn. You're red as a lobster and with that fair skin you're going to be in trouble."

She and her husband drifted toward their trailer, Bateson walking slowly. No one was left but the young mother with the small boy, the sandy-haired man, the manager and myself. I had a suspicion that the manager was lingering in order to see how fast the acquaintance between MacIntosh and me was going to develop.

"Sam," Mrs. Miller called, and I saw the small boy had provided himself with pieces of bread, which he was tossing out to the sea gulls. The mongrel dog was now secured by a piece of rope.

"Come on, Hotchkiss," he said.

The dog with the unlikely name had a mind of its own. It took off after a sea gull and everything happened at once. The gull rested mockingly on a wave, Hotchkiss dived into the water, and the small boy dived after him. I dropped my robe and went after Sam, hauling him out with some difficulty because he still clung to the rope.

"Sam," his mother cried in alarm, "are you all right?"

I laughed. "He's a trifle moist but otherwise he's okay."

"Hotchkiss is wet, too," Sam declared. "He'll catch cold."

"We'll dry him off," Mrs. Miller said.

"You can't keep pets in this trailer park, Mrs. Miller." The manager was firm. Nothing seemed to escape that woman's eye.

"Hotchkiss needs me." Sam's hand tightened on the frayed rope.

"He won't bother anyone, Mrs. Thomson, and they've just adopted each other."

"No pets," Mrs. Thomson repeated. "You can't expect nice quiet people like I get, to stay where there's pets. Especially dogs."

"Sam has been ill and he needs something to play with, something to get him out in the sun. Can't you please make an exception?"

"A four-year-old boy is exception enough." Mrs. Thomson turned to take a long look at me, a long look at the man with the scar who had remained in the background all this time. Then she marched back to her cottage and slammed the door as a kind of period to the discussion.

Mrs. Miller's face wasn't laughing now. She was openly dismayed but attempting to speak brightly. "All right, honey, we'll move on before long and find you another dog. One you can keep. I just want to stay here until you have a nice tan."

The little boy dropped the frayed cord and ran back to the trailer, apparently to hide his tears.

"Thank you so much, Miss—" She looked at me inquiringly.

"Mary Quarles."

"—for saving Sam."

"He didn't need much saving, not in two feet of water. He's a darling."

His mother tried to conceal her bursting pride. "A little fretful right now. He's convalescing. That's why we took off for the south, to get him out in the sun. I did hope this place would work out, right on the beach and all. Oh, well," she went on cheerfully, "it's not the way we expected. That beastly woman! It wouldn't have hurt her to let Sam keep the dog. Something to play with. I wonder why disappointments on a vacation always seem worse than they do at home."

"Probably because we don't expect so much at home. But a vacation—part of its charm is what we expect of it, don't you think? We expect—well, the unexpected. Only we expect it to be nice." I had to laugh at myself.

"I know how you feel, but if there's anything nice about that—that harpy, I don't know what it is. My husband was hoping we could go into town tonight and maybe take in a show, but she says she won't do any baby-sitting."

"Why don't you go, anyhow?" I said impulsively. "I haven't anything to do. I'm not a trained baby sitter but I've been looking after sick people practically all my life."

"Do you mean it?" Her face brightened. "It is sort of hard on Tom, you know, feeling I've become more mother than wife."

"I really do mean it."

"Tom thinks I'm unreasonable about baby sitters but it seems to me hardly a day passes without some story about little children who were hurt or died because they were left without supervision."

"You aren't unreasonable at all."

"I can't tell you how grateful we'll both be. And you wouldn't need to come over. We're next door to your Scotty. I'll leave the window open. Just listen for him. Sometimes, since he's been ill, he wakes in the night and I want someone to answer if he calls. We wouldn't be late. Certainly not after midnight."

We settled it then and there and turned back toward the line of trailers, Mrs. Miller hastening on ahead to prepare for her evening out. There were lights in the biggest of the house trailers, streaming out from a picture window, which, at the moment, framed the Browns from Toronto. They were drinking highballs and quarreling; the man scowling, the woman crying.

"Only four hundred," she was saying. "And real mink. Of course, it's secondhand but perfect condition. Practically giving it away. It's not just a coat; it's really an investment."

The man made a short hasty comment and she muttered something of which I caught only the words, "—so stingy." Abruptly they became aware that they were not only visible but audible. Brown started to his feet and closed the curtains with a jerk.

Hotchkiss barked and young Miller came out of their trailer, looked around apprehensively, and tossed the dog some meat. He saw me laughing and made exaggerated signs of caution.

"Thanks for looking out for the offspring tonight."

"Glad to."

He grinned. "Sam is young but he may prove a restraining influence."

"On what?"

"Your admirers. That wolf Brown and the angry Scot."

"Who?"

"Man with the scar. Looks as though someone had tried to chop his head off."

From behind us, MacIntosh said coolly, "Someone did," and he strolled away toward the second of the house trailers.

Young Miller and I exchanged a look in which there was a wild surmise.

"Look here," he said, "are you sure you don't mind being left alone? Something about that guy——"

I laughed. "He won't bother me. He won't have a

chance." I shut the door of Jack's Scotty, stumbled, and switched on the lights. Sonia's bathing bag was lying in the well just inside the door. I was positive that I had left it on the couch when I had put on her bathing suit.

Someone had been in the trailer since I had left it.

5

When I had pulled off the wet bathing suit and put Sonia's dress on again, I realized that the MacIntosh man was right. My shoulders and back burned like fire, and I was grateful that the dress was backless. The slightest touch hurt me.

While I set the table for dinner, my attention was divided between the painful sunburn and my predicament. No money, no car keys, no clothes except for Sonia's borrowed dress. My winter wool I had left at her hotel. Of course, I could telephone collect in the morning and ask her to arrange something, but I had a trapped feeling that was unpleasant.

I tossed the bathing bag out of my way, wondering again who could have been in the trailer—and why. By now I had apparently seen all the people in the park.

First was the cottage in which Mrs. Thomson lived and had her office; Mrs. Thomson who disliked me wholeheartedly. She couldn't have been more suspicious of me if she had lived in Lloydsville. For all her insistent talk about nice people, or perhaps because of it, I felt reasonably sure that she had known comparatively few people who would answer that description. There was something shady about her.

Next was the biggest of the three house trailers, the one occupied by the Browns from Toronto. I was glad that I'd be moving on in the morning. Brown might easily prove to be a nuisance in spite of the tight rein his wife kept on him.

The second house trailer was rented by the sandy-haired man with the colorless eyes and the ugly scar on his neck. I thought about him uneasily, recalling his appraising look when I had first awakened on the beach. Unlike the man Brown's, it had held no admiration, just a detached summing up. Something about me had taken him by surprise.

The third house trailer was unoccupied. One of the travel trailers belonged to the Batesons, the second held the Millers and their small son, the third was Jack's Scotty.

Who, then, had been prowling around it while I was asleep on the beach? And what would anyone want? There was nothing in the Scotty but built-in furniture and the food with which it was stocked. Unless—could the angry Scot be the man to whom I was to deliver Sonia's letter? Curiously, it had been the situation and not the individual I had wondered about. But if she had involved herself with a man like MacIntosh I could better understand that revealing flash of terror. She was incapable of coping with such a man.

Up to now I had been feeling resentful, as though Sonia were making unjustifiable use of me. Now I found myself firmly on her side. It was pointless to go on hoping that she would change, become less trusting about people. Sonia was Sonia and she had been trapped once more. But if MacIntosh was the man who had frightened her, he would find me a different kind of proposition. At that point I felt capable of taking on a whole panzer division single-handed.

For a moment I leaned against the cool wall to soothe my burning back, and heard a tap on the door. Before I could move, MacIntosh, now wearing slacks and a shirt open at the throat, came in, took a look at my flaming shoulders, and held out a bottle of sunburn lotion.

I hurt too much to be proud. "Thank you." I unscrewed the top and squeezed some out on my hand, wincing as I patted it on my shoulders.

"Who are you?" he demanded.

"You heard my name. Mary Quarles."

"Are you Sonia's little sister?"

So this was the man to whom I was to deliver the letter.

"Her cousin."

"Out on the beach I knew by your eyes that you were the wrong girl. Eyes and—other things. Like babysitting and hauling a youngster out of the water without waiting to put on a cap to protect your hair, and pulling on a beach robe when you are looked at. Here, give me that." Without ceremony he took the bottle out of my hand, squeezed cooling lotion on my shoulders. "Turn around."

When I did so, he put more on my bare back. It felt heavenly and, for all his unpleasant manner, he was surprisingly gentle. It was then, while he was behind me, spreading the lotion on my back, that he said, "All right, you might as well give it to me, you know. I'll be here until you do. That's fair warning."

"Of course I'll give it to you," I said angrily. "That's what I am here for."

He laughed. "Now I've heard everything."

I pulled away from him and saw Mrs. Thomson standing in the doorway. "Yeah," she said evilly. "I thought so. Just come up to see if you'd found your car keys. I don't like goings-on in this trailer park." She was still staring at us when she backed out. She wouldn't have looked much different if she had caught us in flagrante delicto. I felt as though something unclean had touched me.

"What's that about lost car keys?" MacIntosh asked.

I didn't answer.

"You've lost your car keys?" he repeated, and it occurred to me that he'd persist until he got a reply.

"The one in the door and the one in the Hide-a-Key box. And I rather imagine you took them yourself." Which was asking for trouble.

"Well, well." His mocking tone enraged me.

"From now on you've got me to deal with, and don't make any mistake about that."

"So I was beginning to realize." He sounded rather amused.

"I don't know what you are trying to do to Sonia except for scaring her out of her wits, but you can't scare me." It infuriated me to hear the tremor in my voice.

For a moment his arm tightened around my shoulders, hurting me. He gave a strangled laugh. "You're scared silly." He saw that he was hurting me, said "sorry" in an absent-minded way. "What's that about scaring Sonia?"

"You ought to know. I've never seen her like that. Taking advantage because she's so trusting, so good."

His wasn't a face that revealed much of his thoughts. A hard, tight-lipped face with the ruddy Scots complexion that would make him appear young when he was sixty. He was, I realized, a good-looking man and I wondered for a dismayed moment whether Sonia had, before she met Jack, fallen in love with him. There wasn't, it seemed to me, a single dent in his armor, a single weak link. All that softness, that gullibility of hers, would be battered against his unyielding surface.

"Well," he said oddly, "so I frightened Sonia? What makes you think so? Did she tell you?"

"She didn't tell me anything. You must know that much about her. She's loyal. But I saw her face. You've got some hold on her and—"

He leaned back against the wall of the trailer

shaken by that silent laugh of his. "This I never expected to see: a lamb defending a tigress."

I pushed him furiously toward the door, turned back to dig Sonia's letter out of my handbag, flung it at him. He caught it and stepped outside as I pushed the door in his face.

I was so angry it made me feel better. Or perhaps that was the effect of the deliciously cool lotion on my burned shoulders and back. It was a long time since I had eaten and the cool air made me hungry. When the sun set, the temperature had dropped at least fifteen degrees. I checked the food and planned dinner. Every now and then I found myself turning swiftly to peer out of the windows. The night sounds here were unfamiliar and it seemed to me that someone was moving around outside. I told myself firmly that it was only Hotchkiss in search of another handout.

The fifth match had burned out without lighting the gas and I was muttering to myself in exasperation when someone knocked at the door. The young man outside grinned at me.

"My name is Paxton. I understand you are a tenderfoot. As an inveterate Boy Scout, I dropped by to see if you need any help. I'm in one of those house trailers."

"Do you know how these stoves work? I can't get the blasted thing lighted."

He came in, inspected the two-burner stove and struck a match. Nothing happened. "The gas isn't turned on at the tank. Just a minute." I heard him puttering outside, and then he called cheerfully, "Now try it."

It worked like a charm. "It's all right once you tame it. Thank you."

He leaned against the door frame, stooping a trifle because the trailer wasn't very high. "You'll find people around these places are helpful. Glad to give each other a hand." He looked around. "Gets chilly in the evenings. Do you know how these windows work?"

"I want to leave them open, even if it is a bit cold." I explained about the baby-sitting by remote control.

He had a nice smile. "You see? You've got the hang of trailering already. Where you from?" He wasn't offended when I failed to answer. I was eying in some perplexity the big steak I had found in the icebox and trying to fit it into the small frying pan.

Conversation in a trailer park seems to follow the pattern of the Socratic dialogue. "What brings you here?" I asked.

"Lung collapsed," he said cheerfully. "Wouldn't think it to look at me, would you?"

He had a compact build and a deep tan against which his eyes and hair seemed pale. He wasn't particularly good-looking but he had a good-humored face, and the kind of grooming that succeeds in making a man look casually assured without appearing to be a model for Brooks Brothers' clothes. Unlike most men in Florida, who go in for flamboyant shirts and shorts, he wore beautifully tailored slacks, a pale-gray sports shirt and a light jacket that seemed to be made of Italian silk. It was clear that he liked what he saw of me; it was also clear that he wasn't going to try any passes or to make a nuisance of himself.

"So," he went on, leaning comfortably against the door frame, "the medicos say I'll have to keep out of cold climates from now on. I've been moving from place to place the last couple of months, looking for one that suits me. Then I'll settle down and get back to work. But I'm in no hurry. I like lotus-eating. All that gets me down is the cooking." He looked so pointedly and wistfully at the big steak that I laughed.

"There's enough for two." It had occurred to me that this solid young man would be reassuring to have around if the angry Scot should come back. Defiant as I had been, I acknowledged to myself that, like Sonia, I was afraid of him.

"Now that is the authentic trailer spirit," Paxton said with alacrity. "Suppose I fix a drink while you get to work on that steak. I have a bottle."

I didn't particularly like the idea of Mrs. Thomson seeing him come to my trailer with a bottle. "There's some bourbon. You can have that."

"Fine!"

I stood out of the way while he chopped ice and poured drinks.

"Hey, I'm getting water all over the place," he said apologetically. "Clumsy oaf. There seems to be a leak in the icebox."

"Let it go until after dinner," I suggested. "There's room for only one of us to maneuver in here at a time."

We sipped bourbon and water, sitting at the small table in the front of the trailer, watching the orange afterglow in the sky. Now and then, I got up to look at the steak, to stir the potatoes, to mix a tossed salad.

The Millers came out of their trailer, blinked their car lights, and started off.

"Want another drink?"

"Not for me, but help yourself while I mash the potatoes."

"No, let me do that." He whipped them vigorously until they were fluffy, added a pat of butter and looked proudly at his handiwork. "Some girl is going to get a bargain in me." He slipped, lost his balance, grabbed at the sink. "Oops! We'll have to fix that icebox before you are flooded out. I nearly cut off a hand. That steak knife of yours has an edge like a beheading knife."

That was a cheerful meal. We talked a lot and ate a lot.

"There's some lime pie," I warned him as he began to slice more steak.

"One more serving of steak and then lime pie. I have to keep up my strength, you know."

When we had finished eating, he insisted not only on washing the dishes but on rearranging the shelves on which the dishes and kettles were stacked, and he even straightened out the drawer for the silverware.

"A place for everything and everything in its place," he explained primly when I laughed at him. "One thing about a trailer, it would be hard to lose anything. Or hide anything."

"I don't know about hiding but I've managed to lose my car key. Two of them, as a matter of fact." I explained that, without them, I was stuck at the trailer park.

"From my point of view that is pure gain," he declared, "but it's queer."

"Very queer," I agreed. "Maddening."

Somewhat to my surprise he took the loss of the keys as seriously as I did. After questioning me like Perry Mason about how I'd happened to leave the key in the lock, he said, "So the manager gave you that bottle and you took it into your trailer and forgot all about the key."

"Not my trailer," I corrected him, though it was beside the point, "Jack Kenyon's trailer. Jack is married to my cousin."

A few more questions brought out the reasons for my spending the night there.

"Do you know this Kenyon well?" When I explained that I had met him that day for the first time, he didn't attempt to hide his uneasiness. "I don't like this setup, Miss Quarles. Frankly, it stinks. Do you scare easily?"

"No," I lied. "Why?"

"Well, in the first place, there are lots of vacancies in town. Even the hotel isn't filled to capacity. In the second place, there was someone prowling around a while ago. That is the real reason I dropped by. Heard you were a girl alone and I thought I'd better take a look. I didn't know whether it was accident or wolves or what." He had an engaging smile. "Personally, I'd like to have you stay on but I'm the unselfish type. If you have a flashlight, I'll take a look around outside; see if I can find those keys for you."

There was a flashlight on the shelf over the small sink and he took it and went out. For a few minutes I watched the light moving around the Renault and then over the sand in which the car was parked. Once it swung in an arc and he said in a startled voice, "Who's that?"

There was no answer and he stood moving the flashlight back and forth in a wide semicircle, but there was no one.

My feet were wet and I realized that the leak from the icebox had made the thing overflow. I mopped up the water on the floor and then opened the box. Icy water sloshed over my feet as I pulled out the food and tried to shift the ice. I could hear young Paxton beside the trailer now and the metallic sound when the flashlight knocked against it.

"Any luck?" I called.

"Not so far. I thought the keys might have fallen under the trailer."

"The one in the Hide-a-Key box, too?" I puffed breathlessly. I had got my hands around a block of ice and tugged it out, lifting it into the sink where it fell with a bang.

"Never can tell. Hey"—as the ice thudded in the sink—"what's going on in there?"

"I'm trying to find out what's causing that leak."

I mopped up the water and felt around for the drain. There wasn't enough light to see, and Paxton had the only flashlight, but obviously the thing was clogged. I got a long toasting fork and poked it into the drain. It wouldn't go down. I tried again, pulled out the fork, and light glittered on the thing dangling from it. In disbelief I pulled it up, a necklace that blazed in the light. Only real diamonds could sparkle like that.

"My God! What have you got there?"

I turned to see Paxton standing in the doorway, staring at the necklace.

"Believe it or not, that's what clogged up the drain."

He took it from me, let it run through his fingers, spread it out along his sleeve. The thin chain was of platinum and the diamonds were exquisitely set, and seemed, to my inexperienced eyes, to be flawless. I'd never seen anything like it in my life.

As I slipped in water again, I bent to wipe out the icebox. "Will you help me?"

Young Paxton, who was still staring at the necklace, set it down carefully on the drainboard and lifted the block of ice back into the box and replaced the food. Then he picked up the necklace again.

"Do you always hide your jewelry that way?"

"This isn't mine!"

"Finders keepers," he said lightly.

"Don't be ridiculous."

"There's nothing ridiculous about diamonds. Do you know anything about jewelry?"

I shook my head.

"This thing must be worth close to a hundred thousand dollars." He held it up, fascinated by the many-colored glitter when the light touched it. "Quite a find. I wonder if diamonds live in my icebox. I'll have to find out."

"This is no joke. How on earth did it get there?" I demanded.

"You'll have to ask this—Kenyon, isn't it?—who owns the trailer. Maybe he sent you here as a watch-dog."

"Jack Kenyon couldn't buy a thing like that," I scoffed. "It's silly even to imagine that he could."

"Even sillier," he said mildly, "to deposit a diamond necklace in someone else's icebox. And there are ways of acquiring diamonds without buying them.

What are you going to do about this? Advertise in the Lost and Found?"

"I don't know," I said blankly. "I don't know what to do."

6

Somewhere a dog was barking furiously. Paxton was instantly alert. "Someone out there," he said, his voice low, "and the curtains are wide open. Anyone could have seen that necklace."

The barking was louder, sharper. Someone blundered against the trailer and sheered off with a stifled oath.

"Keep back from that window," Paxton said when I tried to peer out into the dark.

The barking stopped abruptly.

"He must have gone," I whispered.

From the next trailer came a whimper and then Sam called, "Mother!" After a pause he said, "Hotchkiss needs me." When there was no answer his voice rose in alarm. "Mother?"

"Where are you going?" Paxton demanded.

"That's the little boy I promised to look out for. I have to go."

"Better stay where you are. I keep telling you that we've got a prowler."

"All the more reason for not leaving that child alone," I reminded him, saw the door of the Miller trailer open, a small pajama-clad figure outlined against the light, heard him call, "Hotchkiss!"

I caught up the flashlight. For a moment, standing in the door of the Scotty, I felt uncomfortably exposed. Then I ran. The Millers' trailer was empty.

"Sam?" I called.

"Hotchkiss!" I heard the child shout in a kind of counterpoint. "It's me, Hotchkiss."

"Sam! Come back!" The night was black and the stars were incredible. Only for two nights on my way south had I ever seen them so large, so near. Then I switched on the light and ran toward the sound of lapping water.

The flashlight picked up a small dark form huddled on the sand. I bent over and caught a breath of relief. It wasn't Sam; it was the little dog.

"Hotchkiss!" I said, but it didn't move. The little dog was still warm but it was quite dead. My hand was sticky. So was the dog's head.

I found myself shaking with rage. Then I thought of Sam. Anyone who would do that to a little dog—I began to run.

"Sam!" I swung the flashlight from side to side. "Sam! Where are you?"

"Mother!" he called shrilly, panic in his voice. The light found him, up to his thighs in water. He turned, slipped, went down.

I moved as fast as I could, the flashlight prodding the surf in vain. Then I saw a hand, an arm, and plunged into the cold water. The tide was coming in and the water was higher than it had been that afternoon. Rougher, too. I waded up to my waist, swinging the flashlight, calling. Then I was swimming, diving down, clawing at the sandy bottom, coming up for air to shout. There was no answer.

This was not the moment to remember what had happened to Hotchkiss, to let panic take hold of me. The essential point was to be methodical, to search the sand as thoroughly as I could. A four-year-old boy took up so little space.

The moment when my groping hands touched him was the sweetest of my life. I hauled him up, swam back to shore, and laid him on the sand. I began to lift and relax, counting slowly, determined not to lose my head or to hurry things. Two long minutes passed, three. Sam choked, I held him while water gushed from his mouth, and then, with a whimper, he was sick.

After that, I gathered him up, his arms tight around my neck, and carried him back. In the trailer I wanted first of all to get him dry and warm but his arms clung to me so tightly I thought it was better to wait. Physical comfort could come in time but his immediate, overwhelming need was for reassurance. So I held him with that twist of the heart experienced by every childless woman who holds in her arms a child who needs her.

Then, when I had coaxed a smile and even a laugh from him, when that convulsive clasp had relaxed, I found towels and clean pajamas, dried him off, and tucked him into bed after toweling his hair. He had been frightened half to death, he had nearly drowned, he had been sick, and now no familiar face, no familiar voice could answer his basic need.

I sat beside his bed, talking quietly, telling him all the stories about the sea and fishes that I could recall, anxious to substitute for his fears some other focus of attention. As his eyelids began to droop, I talked more and more monotonously, my voice sinking until it was almost inaudible, and at length he slept. Once he sobbed in a kind of hiccup.

I don't know how long I sat beside the sleeping child, unwilling to leave him in case he should awaken again. It wasn't until I had sneezed violently a couple of times that I realized I was soaking wet, my hair hanging in damp strands around my face, my dress dripping on the seat and the floor of the Millers' trailer. I'd have to change at once. Then I recalled that the bikini was also wet, and there was nothing to change to.

I got up to look over at Jack's Scotty. The lights were out so I knew that young Paxton had left and I felt a pang of disappointment. I had counted on having him around in case MacIntosh should come back, but it was, after all, unreasonable to expect him to stay after I had gone.

The thought of MacIntosh made me think of the prowler. Someone had deliberately killed poor Hotch-kiss to stop his barking. An ugly, cruel, and pointless bit of brutality. What kind of person would club that poor dog to death? There was only one person who was likely to do it, the angry Scot who had some association with Sonia, who had mistaken me for her until he had seen the color of my eyes.

The necklace seemed to be the obvious explanation for that association. A stolen necklace. It must be a stolen necklace. Neither Sonia nor Jack could have bought it; anyhow, no one would hide a thing like that if it had been legitimately acquired. I couldn't make myself believe that Sonia was guilty of theft but it wasn't hard to accept the fact that she had, with her incurable gullibility, been taken in by a thief.

If she knew of that necklace, her panic was understandable. It wasn't the kind of thing anyone would lose without taking drastic steps to recover it. I'd back Sonia as far as I could but I was damned if I was going to condone theft. It dawned on me that I had run out of the trailer, leaving the necklace with Paxton, a man whom I had never seen before in my life, about whom I knew nothing except that he was pleasant and helpful. But what else could I have done? Snatched it away from him before I answered Sam's call? And if I had been a minute or so later, I might not have found the child until too late.

Paxton would hardly dare pocket the necklace, I told myself. If he tried to escape with it, the police could easily pick up his car. In this scantily populated section it would be difficult for a man to disappear.

Then I recalled that I was not responsible for the necklace, that I still had no idea to whom it belonged, nor who had hidden it in the trailer. One thing I was sure of, I hadn't been intended to find it. Whoever had dropped it into the drain had assumed that it would be well concealed.

But someone else had known or at least suspected that it was there. Someone had searched the trailer that afternoon while I was on the beach. Someone had killed Hotchkiss to silence him. About all I could be sure of was that the prowler, the man who had killed Hotchkiss, was not Paxton, who had been with me while the prowler was around; he had been with me, indeed, at the very moment when the dog had stopped barking.

It could only be MacIntosh; that was what he had meant when he had said he would stay here until I gave "it" to him. Not the letter from Sonia, the necklace. In that case, he would come back. He was bound to come back.

For a long time I sat there in an agony of indecision, not knowing what was the best thing to do. No wonder Sonia had said this was the worst mess she had ever been in. When she had involved herself with Mac-Intosh she had gone beyond her depth. I began to understand her terror of having Jack find out. He wasn't the man to stand by if Sonia were publicly linked with theft. In Jack's profession, adverse publicity was fatal and I couldn't see him sacrificing his career for Sonia or for anyone else. Jack was for "me first."

The idea grew slowly. If I were to hide the necklace and then see that it was turned over to the police with some story of having found it in the water or on the sand, the risk of Sonia being involved would be diminished if not eradicated.

I never liked anything less than the idea of going back to Jack's trailer. A small sleeping boy was no protection but I felt more secure in there; at least no hidden fortune in jewels was lurking to attract prowlers. Prowlers—or worse. The killing of that dog had been ruthless and unnecessary, a deliberately vicious thing.

I looked at my watch. It was only ten o'clock. The Millers could hardly be back for another two hours. Sam was deeply and peacefully asleep. Only a slight patch of moisture that had darkened his hair remained from his experience. I pulled myself together and looked around for my flashlight, but I had dropped it on the beach when I went into the water after Sam. I let myself out of the trailer and walked slowly over to Jack's Scotty.

For a moment I stood looking up at that incredible sky. There wasn't a sound but the rhythmic lapping of the water, not a movement except for the intermittent flash from a distant lighthouse. Then a television program blasted on in the Browns' big house trailer and something near me moved away in the sand, a movement that I sensed rather than heard.

I realized that I had been clearly visible when I came out of the lighted trailer and made a dash for the Scotty, fumbled for the door, opened it and went inside, pulling the door shut behind me.

I stood in the dark, hesitant about turning on the lights because the curtains had not been drawn. In the blackness of the night I might as well be on a lighted stage.

I decided not to turn on the lights. I wouldn't even attempt to make up the couch bed. I'd just take off the wet dress, dry myself as well as I could, and lie down until morning. Then—well, what then? When I called Sonia, what would she say or do?

For this time, at least, there could be no pretenses or deceptions between us. I'd have to tell her about the necklace, make her see that I could not condone theft even for her sake. I'd have to persuade her to agree to return the money Jack had borrowed from me and make some arrangement so that new keys could be obtained for the Renault.

And what was I going to tell her about the letter? That I had delivered it to MacIntosh, that I knew, as well as I knew anything, that she could not count on him? A tigress, he had said. He'd made it clear that he hated her guts and that she was no match for him. A lot of bad news would go over that telephone wire in the morning.

For a moment I stood trying to orient myself in the dark. On my right was the raised dining area with a bench on either side of the table. On the left was another raised section with a couch bed. The floor in the middle of the trailer was lower, making a kind of shallow well, so there would be room enough for a man to stand upright. The sink and stove were on the left, the icebox across from it on the opposite wall. The whole thing couldn't be much more than fifteen feet long.

I groped for the edge of the sink on my left to guide me, took a cautious step down into the well, and stepped into warm water. Another step and I struck something soft and yielding. Someone had moved the bathing bag again, I thought, and bent over to pick it up. I touched cloth and then hair and then a face. I jerked back my hand as though it had been scorched and found the light switch.

My first thought was that, after all, young Paxton had not left the trailer. He was lying crumpled up, face down, with the handle of the steak knife protruding from between his shoulders, and the wetness on my shoes was his blood.

7

A hand clamped down on my shoulder and I screamed. Then it slid over my mouth.

"Good God! How did this happen?"

It was the angry Scot, looking down at the motionless body. I had had all I could take. His hand left my mouth, he caught me as I sagged and shoved me onto one of the benches.

"Put your head down. You can't faint now. Where's that drink Mrs. Thomson said you had? Oh, here it is." He splashed bourbon into a glass and held it to my lips. "Drink this," he said like one of those arbitrary creatures in *Alice in Wonderland,* and the liquid dribbled down my chin. He shook my shoulder. "Go ahead. Take a couple of swallows."

I swallowed with difficulty, choked, swallowed again more easily. He set down the bottle and I looked up into his face. I wasn't even frightened now. He had killed poor young Paxton and he would probably kill me, but I waited in a sort of fatalistic calm.

"You'll have to tell me about it," he said, his voice unexpectedly quiet. "There will be all kinds of particular hell to pay and no guessing how long we have." For the first time he noticed that I was soaking wet. Sonia's dress clung to me as though I were naked. "What happened to you?"

"I had to go into the water again to fish out Sam," I said dully. "The dog woke him when it barked." I was shaking; my teeth chattered. His hand tightened on my shoulder and I winced. "You're hurting me."

"Go on," he said, but he dropped his hand.

"Did you have to kill the dog too?" I asked, and began to cry.

He did not answer my question. "So you heard Sam go out and you followed him. How long were you away from the trailer?"

"He nearly drowned. I had to work on him for a few minutes. Then he was sick. Later I waited for him to go to sleep. I couldn't leave him while he was still frightened. He's only a baby. I was with him—oh, perhaps it was half an hour in all."

"And when you came back here—"

"The lights were out. He was here—like that. I—stepped in his blood." My voice shook. "And then you came."

"Do you know him?"

"His name is Paxton. He's renting that house trailer next to yours. He was—so nice. Was the necklace worth all that? A man's life?"

"What necklace?" he asked sharply.

"You don't have to pretend," I said wearily. "I found it."

In the narrow space there was little room to move. He stood looking down at the quiet, huddled body. "Ever see that knife before?"

I looked quickly. Looked away again. "It belongs here. A steak knife. We—used it tonight." My voice rose. "Don't do that. You're not supposed to touch them when they've been murdered. I know that much."

Ignoring my frantic protest he bent over, his hands on those still shoulders. "Quiet. You don't want to bring the whole trailer park down on our heads." Carefully he lifted the head and turned it. "I thought so. You jumped to conclusions. Look here."

"No."

His voice roughened. "Look here, I say."

"I can't." But I could, of course. Incredulously, I stared at the dead face, my hands covering my mouth to smother the scream that tore at my throat. "It's Jack Kenyon."

MacIntosh put the head back as it had been and then, methodically, he went through Jack's pockets, examining everything in them, returning each object. There wasn't, I noticed, a billfold. In a hip pocket there was a small flask. He unscrewed the top, sniffed at it, put it back. Then he got up, slid onto the seat facing me across the small table.

"Now, then, we've got to have a talk. What are you doing here?"

I shook my head.

"What was the idea of giving me that envelope with the blank sheet of paper in it?"

That startled me into speech. "Blank paper!"

"Well, you can talk. I was beginning to wonder." He pulled an envelope out of his pocket and flicked it across the table. "Why did you give me that, and how the hell did you know about me?"

I had edged across the seat and now I groped for the door, opened it and was on my feet all in a flash. Before I could get outside, he had lunged across the table and gripped my wrist.

"You aren't going anywhere." He pulled me around the table onto the bench beside him, slid his arm around my shoulders, holding me against him. "Go on and talk some more."

"I'm not going to tell you anything," I said firmly, though my voice shook treacherously.

"All this for Sonia. I can imagine her protecting you."

"She would."

"Suppose you tell me about that necklace."

I couldn't trust my voice, which betrayed just how frightened I was. At last I asked, "Why did Jack come here? Was he killed for the necklace?"

"What do you know about the necklace?"

I was stubbornly silent.

"You had better tell me, you know. It might keep my mind on my business. Otherwise, looking as you do at this moment—"

That forced words out of me. "I found it when there was a leak in the icebox." I described what had happened.

"So then you ran out, leaving this guy Paxton alone with a diamond necklace. You're a trusting soul, aren't you?"

"If I hadn't gone, the little boy would have drowned. I had no choice."

"No, I suppose, being you, you hadn't."

"Anyone would have done the same thing," I said defensively.

He gave a short laugh. "I notice that Paxton didn't volunteer to answer the child's call. And can you see Kenyon leaving those diamonds to save a little boy?"

"He's dead. Don't talk about him that way. It's not decent."

"Spare me the sentimentality. Death doesn't change a man's character, and Kenyon was a heel of the first water."

"That's no excuse for murder."

"Nothing really is an excuse for murder. But he was asking for it. Spoiling for it. Only he overlooked something. He meant someone else to die and he was too slow on the draw."

"He came here tonight to kill you? Is that what you are asking me to believe? That he planned this?"

"Use your head, woman. It's a cinch Kenyon didn't plan his own murder."

"Are you going to plead self-defense?"

"If I thought there was a chance you'd believe me," he said, "I'd assure you that you will be next. Look here, I've got to find out what you know. Time is running out and—what's your name, anyhow?"

"You've heard it. Mary Quarles."

"All right, Mary. Suppose you listen to my story. Then perhaps you'll tell me yours, unless you are a party to this business and if you are I'll never trust my judgment again. With the body of a Venus you have the nature of—"

"A sheep," I said in resignation. "Yes, I know. That's what Richard says."

"Who is Richard?"

"The man I am going to marry," I told him with a shade of defiance.

"Well," he said cryptically, "it's early days yet. So early that you had better move out of reach over to the other bench."

When I had done so, edging carefully in that narrow space so I need not step down into the well, he looked at me. "Perhaps that was a mistake. Now I can see you better."

He broke off and then went on briskly, "All right. This is the story. My name is Charles MacIntosh, and I'm an attorney. I practice in California. One of my clients is—well, never mind that. She married a wealthy man who keeps a tight rein. If he ever caught her straying off the range, he'd divorce her. Anyhow, recently she spent a few weeks at Las Vegas where she had an affair with Jack Kenyon."

I gave a strangled exclamation.

"Oh, yes, didn't you know? That's the way he has been supplementing his income. Older women fall for him. When they don't pay him sufficiently for—his attentions, he relieves—relieved them of their jewelry."

"No! How hideous. Oh, poor Sonia. What an unspeakable thing, and they've been married only a few months. How could he? If Sonia guessed that—"

"Poor Sonia knew all about it. And there's no evidence that she put up any strenuous objection to his —how shall I put this to save your sensibilities?— earning an honest penny."

"I don't believe you."

"How about shutting up so I can get this across to you?"

It was an ugly story as he told it. Jack Kenyon had worked with a partner who lined up prospective victims who had to have two qualifications: they must be wealthy and they must be vulnerable to publicity so that they dared not prosecute Kenyon when valuable jewelry disappeared, even when they were sure that he had stolen it.

"Easy meat," MacIntosh said. "He had them in a cleft stick. If they opened their traps, they convicted themselves of having given him—let's say unusual opportunities to get his hands on their jewelry. Husbands who held the purse strings could kick them out. Publicity could make fools of them. A very nice racket."

Charles MacIntosh had been called in by his client after Kenyon had stolen her diamond necklace. The theft itself had not triggered her action, because the fool woman had been infatuated. There'd been a time, at least, when she thought he was worth it. But when the papers revealed Kenyon's secret marriage to a young and beautiful woman, she had been beside herself with jealousy and resentment.

MacIntosh had advised her either to cut her losses or to report the theft to her insurance company and the police. Clients hire lawyers to advise them and then pay no attention, like a patient filling a doctor's prescription but not taking the medicine, as though the prescription in itself would do the work. She said she couldn't report it because her husband would raise Cain if he learned of her intimacy with Kenyon, and she wouldn't let it go because she wasn't willing to relinquish the necklace to Sonia.

MacIntosh had had detectives look into Kenyon's background and came on traces of a partner, though it had been impossible to learn the man's identity. Kenyon's contract at Las Vegas was dissolved as a result of the exposure of his marriage. He and Sonia set off in the trailer, a nice anonymous way of traveling until he could dispose of the necklace.

For the first time, I interrupted. "I never understood the trailer. It's not like Sonia at all."

"How right you are!" he said dryly. "But after Kenyon's contract was broken, he had to pick up small jobs in obscure resorts, and the two of them, unless I'm mighty mistaken, were practically flat broke. What they made easily they spent easily, and the trailer always provided a cheap way of life in between jobs. My own guess is that they kept this thing out of sight, partly because it's not the way glamorous stars live and partly because they were afraid."

"Of the police?"

"Of Kenyon's partner. There must have been a break between them because, since his dealings with my client, Kenyon doesn't seem to have been operating at the old stand. There's a chance that, after she married him, Sonia objected to a two-way split."

I'd been half-credulous, but this idea was so revolting that I balked at accepting it. "You're just guessing."

"Up to a point," he agreed. "But the possibility of a double cross strikes me as inescapable. The Kenyons were mighty careful about that marriage. They didn't want it to leak out. Only someone close to them could have known about it, someone resentful enough against Kenyon to expose it. I can't see them confiding about that marriage in anyone except the partner, whom it would concern."

MacIntosh had learned about the Scotty, traced it to the Florida trailer park. When he saw me on the beach he assumed I was Sonia until he got a look at my eyes, which were the wrong color. And there had been other things, details that did not fit what he knew about Sonia. I had gone into the water to save Sam and had offered to baby-sit for him. I had wrapped up in a beach robe when I was looked at, something, MacIntosh assured me, that would never have occurred to Sonia.

"You searched this trailer while I was on the beach,

didn't you?" I accused him. "You were looking for the
necklace."

"I never entered it until I came with that sunburn
lotion."

"And the dog?"

When I had told him about Hotchkiss he shook his
head. "I remember the dog. Mrs. Thomson wouldn't
let the Millers keep it. I heard a dog barking somewhere. That was probably when Kenyon was closing in.
He must have killed the poor beast."

"And who killed Jack?"

"The only one with a motive I can see is the partner," MacIntosh said promptly. "The necklace isn't on
Kenyon. I looked."

"I saw you."

He grinned at me. "I think we'll have to make a
search for your pleasant friend Paxton."

"I don't believe it."

"I thought at first the partner might be Brown, who
was definitely trying to make contact with you out on
the beach. He was up to something. But I guess he
just had other ideas."

I sneezed violently and groped for a handkerchief.
He put a clean one in my hand. "You had better get
out of those wet clothes before you have pneumonia."

"There's nothing to change into except Sonia's bikini and, anyhow, that's wet, too. I didn't bring a
wardrobe with me. I planned to buy what I needed
after I got to Florida."

"You've got to get out of those clothes. There must
be something—"

"Wait," I exclaimed suddenly, "none of this makes
sense. For a moment I almost believed you."

"Well, thanks."

"Sonia and Jack would not have practically forced
me to come here if they had known Jack's partner
would show up."

"Wouldn t they? What did bring you here?"

I explained about Sonia's telephone call and that it

had come at a time when I was fed up with Lloydsville and wanted to get away. I had packed a weekend
bag and set off the next morning.

"Why were you fed up?"

To my own surprise I told him about my humiliating
experience at the country club.

"Did Sonia know about this experience of yours?"

"No."

"What triggered her call?"

"The weather reports from up north."

"Nuts," he said inelegantly. "What had happened to
you before that?"

"Nothing ever happens to me."

"That's all over now. Go on. Something must have
happened."

"Aunt Jane died and I was going to marry Richard
Burgess."

"And how did Richard affect the situation?"

"He didn't really. But Sonia thought he was prejudiced against her."

"And how did Aunt Jane's death affect the situation?" When I made no comment, he said casually,
"Did she have something to leave?"

"That wouldn't mean a thing to Sonia, not a thing.
I told her this afternoon I wanted to share, right now
if she needed it. But she said no."

"No—what?"

"That there wasn't really enough for more than one
of us."

"How would Richard have felt about you sharing
with Sonia?"

Again I made no comment.

He was silent for a long time. "Now I think you had
better explain why you gave me the envelope."

When I had told him, he said grimly, "Do you begin
to get it now?"

I shook my head.

"Aunt Jane dies, leaving you her money. Then you
plan to marry Richard Burgess who, sensible man,

doesn't like Sonia. So she plans to get her hands on that inheritance before Richard can prevent you from being too open-handed. A nasty trick is played on you so that you'll be set up in your home town as a lush. Sonia gets you down here and, when you balk at coming to the trailer park, she gives you that phony letter to deliver."

"But—"

"Wait," he said impatiently. "Let's look at the picture and see what sense it makes. You're sent out here. Why? Not to deliver that letter. That's out. So what else is there? A diamond necklace over which Kenyon is in real trouble. He's held out on his partner who, in turn, has retaliated by revealing his marriage. Kenyon knows the partner has, in effect, said, 'You can't do this to me.'

"It dawns on the Kenyons that as long as the partner is around he is in a position to blow them sky-high. So they plan to get rid of him. They dangle the necklace before his nose like the proverbial carrot before the donkey. The partner is to come to the Scotty looking for the necklace, he is to die, and little Mary Quarles, filled with alcohol and dope, will have her fingerprints on the weapon that killed him. Drunken rage? Defending your virtue? It wouldn't matter."

"But I could prove—"

He reached over and raised my chin, making me look at him. "No one ever inherited from a healthy young woman," he said at last.

"You mean I was supposed to be killed, too? That if Jack hadn't died first, I'd have been killed?"

"That's my case for the jury," he said.

"No," I whispered after a long, long time. "No, Sonia wouldn't do that to me."

"Your cousin Sonia," he said deliberately, "is a beautiful woman, though she's not a patch on you, and why you haven't discovered that for yourself eludes me. Nothing but a dead body would keep my mind off yours, and at that it's a struggle. But your cousin Sonia is also a prize witch and you are a thoroughly nice girl, Mary. Try as you will, you can't conceal it."

"It's so ridiculously complicated," I protested. "No one would ever believe I would kill a man."

"You were to be drunk. Remember? If I don't miss my guess, that flask in Kenyon's pocket is nicely laced with dope of some kind. After all, it worked once before in Lloydsville."

"But why bring a doped flask when Jack had already publicly left the bottle of bourbon for me with Mrs. Thomson?"

"That's why. Nothing must be wrong with that one. Its purpose was to set you up as a problem drinker." He squeezed out from behind the table.

"What are you going to do?" I demanded.

"I've got to get the police. Mrs. Thomson has a telephone. As a lawyer I am perfectly aware that I should have called them three-quarters of an hour ago. But I had to get things straight with you first. Find out the score." He hesitated for a moment. "I don't like leaving you here alone. Come with me."

I'd never wanted anything less than I wanted to stay in the trailer with Jack Kenyon's dead body, but I had promised to keep an eye on Sam. I didn't dare risk having him awaken again and get no answer if he called. I told Charles so.

"The boy will be all right. He's not likely to wake up again after all he's been through tonight."

"I promised."

"And you always keep your promises? That's nice to know. I'll remember it. Lock that door and don't open it unless you recognize my voice."

I nodded.

He hesitated. "Sure you'll be all right?"

I nodded again, summoned up a smile. "I'm sure. Only hurry."

"You're a gallant little devil, Mary." He pulled me into his arms, kissed me hard on the mouth. "My seal," he explained, "to protect you until I get back."

For a moment we looked at each other, the air highly charged between us. He reached for me again and then he laughed, his arms dropped, and he opened the door.

"Lock it," he said, and went outside.

I stood staring at the door. I heard him say, an edge of impatience in his voice, "Lock it!" and moved to shove home the bolt.

8

He had not been gone five minutes before I heard the tap at the door. I sat unmoving, holding my breath, my heart sounding loud in the room.

"Mary?" It was a whisper.

I reached for the lock and then my hand dropped, distrustful of that anonymous whisper. He spoke in a low tone and I recognized his voice. He stood outside the door with Mrs. Thomson behind him.

"She didn't believe me," he said grimly, "and she wouldn't let me use her telephone." He stood to one side then, so the woman could come in. "All right, take a look but make it fast. The police must be informed at once."

She was rigid with shock when she saw the body. Then, moving with surprising quickness, she was inside. She bent over, saw his face. "Mr. Kenyon! It's Mr. Kenyon!" The color drained out of her face, the loose mouth writhed. "Kilt. He's been kilt. I'm not," she said absurdly enough, "going to have a murder in this park."

"You've got a murder," Charles reminded her. "Now that you are satisfied, get on the telephone and call the police."

"I'm not going to get mixed up with the police. It would give this place a bad name. I won't have it."

Her reaction was so preposterous that I almost laughed. Then I saw Charles's strangely colorless eyes appraise her.

"Got a record?" he asked.

"Don't you dare say that. I could sue you for that. This is a nice respectable trailer park. We've never had the police here." Her voice was shrill. She was beginning to shake again. "Do something!" she ordered Charles. "You've gotta do something. We have to get him out of here."

In her dithering panic she seized Jack's arm, tugged at it. She would have attempted to drag that dead body out of the trailer if Charles had not restrained her by main force, holding her arms clamped against her sides. She struggled against him in a frenzy, her face distorted, while Charles refused to relax his grip. I noticed again what a hard face he had. She might as well have battered against a stone wall. Eventually she became aware of this herself, and she relaxed, sagging against the table.

"What are we going to do?" she asked dully.

"This is murder, Mrs. Thomson, like it or not. We must have the police here without delay or we'll all be in real trouble. And that goes for you, too."

"I'm not going to get mixed up in it." King Canute holding back the tide.

"You are mixed up in it. I'm a lawyer and I know what I'm talking about." His authoritative tone cut through her panic, steadied her.

"Murder," she said slowly, "and a lawyer." The watery eyes crawled like something unclean over my body that was so starkly outlined by the wet dress. "You got a lawyer right on the spot, Miss Quarles, so's you can get away with it. Killing that nice Mr. Kenyon after all he's done for you. Taking care of your trailer, keeping an eye on you when you've been drunk so's you'd be all right. I told him that first day he was wasting his time on a lush, but he said it was for his wife's sake. Said she was fond of you and felt responsible."

"Miss Quarles never met Jack Kenyon until today," Charles told her. "She never saw this trailer until this afternoon."

Mrs. Thomson laughed. "Yeah? She's been here, off and on, for three days. Most of the time she was sleeping it off or acting just plain mean."

"That wasn't Mary."

"Another girl that Mr. Kenyon called Mary? Another girl in the self-same dress and bikini and dark glasses with those shiny triangular frames? Another girl with the same face and figure? You aren't getting away with a thing, mister. She kilt him, and that's the story I tell the police if you get them here."

I think she actually believed he would cave in under her threat, that he would connive in attempting to cover up Jack's murder. Instead, he told her, "You're going back to use your telephone. And you're going now."

"I'll tell the police she did it." She repeated the phrase as though it were some magic formula.

"Go right ahead and tell them whatever you damned well please. But Mary was framed. She didn't kill Kenyon."

"And who did? You, maybe?"

"I think he was probably killed by Paxton."

The watery eyes blinked. "Paxton?" she repeated blankly.

"Man who rents that house trailer next to mine."

"No one rents that trailer. It's been empty since the hurricane last fall. And I never heard of a man named Paxton."

"But he told me——" I began, saw Charles's warning gesture, and broke off.

Mrs. Thomson looked at Charles. "You ever see this guy she is talking about?"

"No," he said slowly, "I never saw him."

She flashed me a look of triumph, turned challengingly to Charles. "So it's just the girl's story. What do we do now?"

"You call the police at once or you'll be in more trouble than you ever dreamed of."

"You staying here?"

"You're damned right I'm staying here. There's a killer around, Mrs. Thomson.

"Yeah," She looked from Jack's still body to me, and then she scuttled out into the dark.

Charles's face was grim as he followed her with his eyes. He reached out to draw the curtains. "We can be seen from outside."

"Jack, too?"

"No, not unless someone stood right against the window and looked down."

"She really thinks I killed him," I said at last, as though speaking the words aloud would make them credible.

He did not attempt to deny it, or to soften the situation. "That's the way it has been set up. This was a very carefully planned operation, Mary. All that went wrong was that Kenyon was caught in his own trap."

"She'll tell the police I did it, that there isn't any such man as Paxton, that I've been here for three days, drunk and disorderly."

"I rather think Mrs. Thomson is not unknown to the police. That will make a difference in the amount of credence they give any statement of hers."

"But it won't really alter the facts, will it?" When he made no reply, I said unhappily, "It was Sonia who was here this week, impersonating me, wearing the clothes she lent me, letting Jack call her Mary."

"Of course."

Even then, when I was bewildered and frightened, my strongest feeling was one of grief for the loss of Sonia. Part of me still persisted in defending her. You can't love and protect a person for most of your life and then abandon not only your thinking but your feeling about the person. I conjured up a dozen memories of her, warm and affectionate, kind and sweet, basically simple and unspoiled in spite of all the adulation she had received. A born victim.

In the long run I came back to that. Sonia was a born victim. She had been caught up in something she couldn't handle. If she had made unscrupulous use of me, it was because she was frightened, unable to help herself. Some part of my mind cravenly blotted out the possibility that she had wanted me to die so that she could have Aunt Jane's inheritance.

Charles MacIntosh had been watching me through the fluctuations of my thoughts. Now he grinned. "Stop being a little mother to your cousin. Stop protecting her. She's not worth it. Believe me, Mary, she's not worth it."

"At least she wouldn't have killed Jack or had any part in it. Never in the world. She was terribly in love with him."

His voice was sharp, unsympathetic. "Don't try to cover for your cousin. She intended to let you take a murder rap. She set you up for it very carefully. It was a long-range, singularly cold-blooded deal. Just remember that. If her plans had gone through according to schedule, Paxton would be dead and so, my dear, would you. A woman whose last conscious act had been to kill."

In a flash I recalled the conversation I had overheard outside the Kenyons' room: "It's all happening too fast. Everything at once. Suppose they meet?" And Jack's revealing remark, "Whose idea was this in the first place?"

"What is it?" Charles asked, watching my face.

I told him, repeating the conversation as accurately as I could.

"Then stop trying to protect Sonia, for God's sake. Tell the police the exact truth, Mary. Don't try to hold back a single thing."

"And how much do you think they will believe? Honestly, Charles, how much? There's no trace of Paxton. If they dig back, they'll find out that gossip about me being drunk in Lloydsville. Without the necklace there's no motive for anyone else, and the necklace has disappeared, too. There's only my word that it was ever here. What are we going to do?"

"We wait. The police should be here any minute. Why don't you lie down?"

I looked at the couch bed at the other end of the trailer, but I'd have had to squeeze past Jack or step on him to reach it, which was unthinkable. In that little Scotty the body seemed awfully big.

Charles pulled me down beside him. "You'll have a bout of pneumonia unless you change those clothes. There are sweaters and extra slacks in my suitcase. Much too big but at least they are dry. I'll get them."

I clutched at his arm in sudden panic. "No, don't go."

"Okay, you've asked for it." He held me against him, kissing me from my forehead to my chin, quick, light kisses. Then abruptly he pushed me away. "The other side of the table for you. This is no time to start something I can't finish."

"This is no place for it, either, not with Jack there." Sitting on the opposite bench, pushing wet hair out of my eyes, I planted my elbows on the table, my chin in my cupped hands, careful not to look in Jack's direction.

"Do you ever read Emily Dickinson?" he asked me unexpectedly. "There's a line of hers somewhere: 'Dying is a wild night and a new road.' You might try to think of it like that."

"A wild night," I agreed, "in spades. But the new road?"

Something in his expression enlightened me, and at the same time I said hastily, "I didn't know that men ever read women poets."

He grinned, as much at my evasion as at my comment. "Just novels with hard hitting, and harder drinking, tough heroes and easy blondes? That's romantic escape for them as hasn't had it. Never rely on a guy who has to flex his muscles vicariously."

"What kind would you recommend?" I was fully aware that he was trying desperately to drag my attention away from Jack.

"You might try me," he suggested.

"Somehow," I said, striving for a light tone, "you don't inspire confidence."

"It's that scar. Doesn't do me justice."

"How did you get it? You told Mr. Miller someone tried to chop your head off."

"Actually, that was true. Someone did. In Korea. But I had other ideas." He dropped his light tone as my eyes, in spite of myself, went back to Jack. "Believe me, Mary, if he were here, and you were where he is now, he wouldn't be wasting a thought on you. He'd be worrying about himself."

"Don't make any mistake about it, Charles. That's exactly what I am doing—worrying about myself. Are they going to arrest me?"

"They'll have to question you, of course." He was speaking absently as though his mind wasn't on what he was saying.

"What's worrying you?"

"How much time has Mrs. Thomson had?"

"I don't know. A quarter of an hour, maybe a little more. Why?"

"The police should have come by now." He got up from behind the table, moving carefully so as not to step on Jack. "I don't believe that fool woman ever called them. She's had dealings with the law before. Probably," and he grinned at me, "what she was so quick to expect when she found me in here putting sunburn lotion on your extremely beautiful back." He laid his hand on my shoulder.

"Where are you going?" I demanded.

He heard the terror in my voice. His hand tightened. "I've got to get the police, Mary. Nothing else to do. As it is, we're going to have hell's own time explaining the delay."

"But suppose Mrs. Thomson refuses to let you use her telephone?"

"Then I'll drive to the nearest house. There are

more places than you may realize scattered along the beach."

I've always rather despised clinging vines but I was one at that moment. I couldn't leave because of Sam and I didn't want to be left alone because of Jack.

"Please, please, don't go. The Millers will be back before long. They'll get the police for us."

"Damn it, don't make this harder than it is, darling. There's bound to be a telephone somewhere nearby. I won't be a moment longer than I can help. Just don't open the door until I come back. You'll be safe. I swear you'll be safe. But don't try to be brave. If anyone attempts to get in, keep the door locked and scream bloody murder."

On that encouraging note he took a long look at me and closed the door behind him. This time I didn't have to be reminded to lock it.

At first I switched out the lights. Then, because I was morbidly aware of Jack's still presence, I turned them on again and tried to control my shivering by concentrating on what had happened, on trying to disentangle it.

The unbearable part was trying to fit Sonia into a new pattern, with every memory of her distorted, made incredibly ugly. If Charles were right, Sonia had, from the moment Aunt Jane died, planned to get rid of me so that she could seize the inheritance I would so gladly have shared with her.

She had, with Jack's help, arranged for Gus to give me a doped drink and to inform the Town Crier that I was drunk and disorderly. She had set up a picture of me, again drunk and disorderly, at the trailer park, and then sent me there, dressed in clothes she had made familiar, to be a murder suspect when a man was killed in the trailer, and then, presumably, to die of an overdose of drugs.

I remembered how she had changed my hair style, made up my eyes, altered my appearance so that, even to myself, I had looked like Sonia Colette.

It was unspeakable. It was unbelievable that she had so much evil in her. Little by little, I realized that I simply didn't believe it. Charles had sounded so convincing that I had accepted what he told me. Everything Sonia had done could be explained quite innocently.

All this time my ears were straining for the sound of footsteps, for the sound of a motor. If Mrs. Thomson had let Charles use her telephone, he should be back by now. If she hadn't, he should be starting his car.

There wasn't a sound but the surf beating as though it were the heart of the world. That was when the ugly suspicion began to grow that he did not intend to call the police, that he did not intend to come back. I had believed his story because, in spite of myself, I had liked him. Liked him? I had fallen headlong as though I'd tumbled down a waterfall.

After all, this wasn't so unnatural. I hadn't had much experience with men who seemed to admire me. While Sonia was around, no one had ever noticed me; since she had left Lloydsville. I had been little more than Aunt Jane's sick-room attendant, with almost no opportunity to meet young men and none whatever to develop any friendship with them. Any social engagement of mine was followed, invariably, by a heart attack of Aunt Jane's. Against a man like Charles MacIntosh, good-looking, experienced, as attractive for the qualities that seemed mysterious as for those I recognized, I had had exactly no chance at all.

Now he had gone off and he probably had the diamond necklace in his pocket.

But if he had actually gone, escaped with the necklace, that departure of his would be tantamount to a confession of guilt. Even Mrs. Thomson could not deny he had been there as she had denied any knowledge of Paxton. And other people had seen him: the Batesons and the Millers. Somehow, this wasn't as consoling a thought as it should have been. It wasn't enough to be cleared of any complicity in Jack's murder. I wanted Charles to be cleared, too.

Stupidly susceptible and childishly vulnerable I might be to Charles's love-making, but the knowledge remained that I had fallen in love with him. And he wasn't, as I was still sane enough to be clearly aware, the nice young man that Paxton so obviously was.

What had become of Paxton? According to Charles, he was probably Jack's partner, and Jack with Sonia's help had intended to eliminate him, leaving me to take the blame. Paxton had obviously lied to me when he had said that he was renting one of the trailers, but there could be an innocent explanation for that. I tried to picture him stabbing Jack, escaping with the necklace.

But he hadn't, I remembered, killed the little dog. It wasn't credible that, in the small trailer park, there were two brutal killers. Not, I supposed, that the death of Hotchkiss could be compared with that of Jack, but it had been a vicious action.

Suppose that Paxton had not gone away, taking the necklace with him. Suppose that Jack's murderer had killed him, too. That left Charles. There was no one else but Charles.

"Mary," Charles said quietly, and with a sob of relief I opened the door, letting the nightmare dissolve in the air like smoke. He came in, bringing with him a strong smell of gasoline.

"Did you get the police? Are they coming?"

"I haven't called them yet. Mrs. Thomson refused to let me in. She sounds absolutely scatty with terror. I tried to start my car, but someone has slashed all four tires. Not only that; the Batesons' car has been drained of gas. I slipped in a pool of it. And with your car keys missing—"

"What about the Browns?"

"They were in the midst of the grandfather of all rows when I knocked. I heard Mrs. Brown scream at him not to open the door but I finally talked him over. He explained that his wife had a bad attack of the jitters, that she was sure someone was prowling and she was trying to persuade him that they must leave right away. She made clear she had wanted to go to a smart hotel at Miami Beach in the first place and then, and I quote, the cheap skate rented a house trailer at this dump. I asked if I could borrow their car for half an hour because I wanted to get the police."

Seeing the question in my face, he said, "No, I didn't tell them about Kenyon. But the word police was bad enough. Mrs. Brown broke in before he could say anything. She was wild, said that settled it, they were getting out at once."

"But they can't do that," I said blankly. "What's the matter with them?"

He grinned. "You haven't caught up with that combination yet, have you? Her jealousy of you on the beach, her fear of the police, her alarm at the idea of any resulting publicity."

"Oh, you mean they aren't married?"

"They are probably married but not to each other. The affair has already begun to sour and I suspect that she has burned her bridges and she can't go back."

"What do we do now?" It seemed to me that question had been tossed back and forth for hours.

He shrugged. "We wait for the Millers. Without a car—"

"But Jack Kenyon must have had a car. And Paxton, too. Neither of them could have walked here. Where are they?"

"God knows where Kenyon's car is. I haven't seen a trace of it. So far as Paxton is concerned, if I am right about him, he is as far away from here as he can get." There was a startled expression on his face. "Or —perhaps not."

"What is worrying you?"

"If Paxton killed Kenyon—and I can't see any alternative, can you?—then he won't dare leave just yet. He's bound to be around somewhere."

"I can't see any sense in that."

"Unfinished business," he said grimly. "This is a murder rap and you are the only one who can identify him." After a moment he said, "Don't look like that. I shouldn't have told you."

"Would it help not to know? Would ignorance make me any safer? Anyhow, I'm in this now and we have to do something. You've got to tell the Browns about the murder, Charles. After all, it won't be exactly a secret after the police come, will it?"

"I suppose not." He sounded dissatisfied. After being so hell-bent on getting the police, I had the curious feeling that he no longer wanted them. "I don't like it, Mary. This situation has been set up for you. I don't like leaving you alone. I have the damndest hunch that something is going to happen."

"Something has already happened."

"Okay. I'll be on my way. I'll walk until I find a telephone. The problem is that country people go to bed early. Without lights it would be easy to pass a house and not even know it was there. I don't know how long I'll be gone. Stay here. Understand?"

"I understand."

Something in my voice alerted him. "Promise?"

After a long pause I said, "No, I'm not going to promise."

9

Moment by moment, I expected the sound of a siren, but no one came. I sat crouched on the seat, waiting and listening, trying not to look at Jack's body.

Whatever Sonia had meant to do, she had not helped to plan Jack's death. She had been genuinely in love with him.

And Paxton? I went back over my meeting with him, the easy gaiety of our dinner, his unobtrusive helpfulness, his inexplicable disappearance, Mrs. Thomson's denial that he had ever been in the park. I found it hard to believe that he was a thief, let alone a murderer. Somehow, it was easier to see Charles MacIntosh killing someone.

One thing was certain. There had been someone else prowling around while Paxton was with me. It was the prowler, not Paxton, who had killed the little dog. On the other hand, Paxton could have known about the necklace. He could have been searching the trailer systematically while he was straightening up after dinner, going through cupboards and drawers. And he had said something about it being difficult to hide anything in a trailer.

Which one was lying: Paxton or Charles?

Time crawled by and Charles still had not come back nor had the police appeared. He had warned me to stay in the Scotty. I was in an agony of indecision. If he had told me the truth, my wisest move would be to stay where I was, safe behind a locked door. But if he had lied—and if he had told the truth—why hadn't

he returned? Why hadn't the police appeared?—I was
left holding the baby. The way it had been set up for
me.

I went over the story Charles had told me but there
was no evidence to support it. He had known about
the necklace on his own admission. He was, in some
respects, a violent man. And what had happened to
Paxton? Why, if he was in the clear, had he lied
about renting the house trailer? And where was he
now?

For some time I had been aware that the wind was
rising. Now, a sudden gust shook the Scotty and the
jar made Jack's body slide and slip toward me as
though it were alive. One hand seemed to grope toward me as though for help. That was the deciding
factor.

I swung open the door, slid off the bench, and
plunged onto into the darkness, closing the door behind me. A brisk wind cut through my wet dress and
made me shiver. For a moment I stood beside the
Millers' trailer, listening, but there was no sound. Sam
was still asleep.

There was no light at the Batesons'. For a moment
I hesitated. She had been friendly; she would at least
let me wait there. I was tempted to knock at the door
and then remembered Mr. Bateson's heart condition. I
dared not awaken him, perhaps startle him.

As I passed their car I stepped in wetness and
smelled gasoline. Perhaps, after all, Charles had told
me the truth. Or had he immobilized the car himself? One thing I learned during that wild night was
that anything is easier to bear than uncertainty, than
not knowing.

I passed the house trailer that young Paxon had
told me he was renting but it was dark and the windows were tightly closed. No car was parked outside.
In contrast, the windows of Charles's trailer were wide
open, the lights were on, the door was ajar. I looked
inside but it was empty. His car, a Mercury, had flat

tires. That much of what he had told me was true. I couldn't see him slashing his own tires unless he had some other means of transportation available.

In the Browns' big house trailer the curtains were securely drawn but the lights were on and the television was going full blast. I knocked on the door.

"Who is it?" Mrs. Brown asked shrilly.

"Mary Quarles."

"What do you want?"

"Let the girl in," Brown said in a tone not to be disobeyed, and she opened it, standing firmly in the doorway, blocking it, looking at me with the same suspicion and hostility that women ordinarily showed to Sonia. It was an odd experience but, in a way, I couldn't blame her, aware of how I must appear with that wet dress clinging to me, starkly outlining every inch of my body. Wasn't it Lady Caroline Lamb who, generations before, had outraged society by appearing in a thin dress, which she had dipped in water, and wearing nothing under it?

"What do you want?" she repeated. She had changed to tight-fitting slacks and sweater, which I coveted, for at least she must be warm.

"May I use your car? It's an emergency."

"Sorry, we are just leaving and we'll be needing it ourselves."

I saw that she had an open suitcase on the floor and several others stacked against the wall, ready for their departure.

"You don't understand," I said desperately. "You can't leave now."

"Why can't we?"

"There's a body in my trailer."

"And whatta body." Brown elbowed his wife to one side. "Whatta body!" He winked at me. "Relax, baby. I'll take care of it."

Unexpectedly his wife dragged him back and slammed the door in my face. "You fool," she screamed, "did you hear what she said? Something's wrong. Get on with your packing. We're getting out of here right now."

"Suppose you let me mind my own business. I give the orders around here."

I didn't like his manner—or his manners—but at least he was going to do something. He would realize that people can't run away from the scene of a murder. He would get the police.

That reminded me that if the police were coming, I'd have to return to the Scotty in order to answer their questions. I had nearly reached it when I heard someone behind me and turned almost into the arms of Mr. Brown. They promptly went around me.

"Well, well," he said softly. "Lovely little Sonia. Think I didn't know you on the beach this afternoon? With a chassis like that?" He pulled me against him, forced my head back, his lips on mine.

I struggled but he only held me tighter. With one hand he began to explore my body and I dug my nails into his face, raking them down. He released me with a yelp of pain, and then savagely jerked me against him again.

Up to now I'd simply regarded him with contempt but now I was afraid of him. "Let me go! Let me go!" I dragged away his groping hand, forced myself free with a sudden pull that almost upset us both.

"What's wrong?" He sounded genuinely surprised and aggrieved. "Just a little fun and games. You playing hard to get? That's not the way I heard it." He gave a fatuous laugh. "Come on, be nice to me, baby. Jack won't mind. Real liberal ideas Jack has. Live and let live, that's Jack."

"What do you want?"

He chuckled. "Always the little businesswoman. That tickled me. A body in the trailer. Like I said, whatta body. But it sure got a rise outta Mabel."

"Mabel?"

He chuckled again. "Oh, just call her Mrs. Brown. For the time being. I brought her along, combining pleasure with business. But not so much pleasure so far. I've been stalling her off, waiting for you to make a move. Now she's set on the idea there's a prowler around and I've had hell's own time keeping her here. All right, baby. Let's take a look."

I stood aside while he opened the door and saw Jack's body sprawled in the well of the Scotty. Then he reached out to haul me inside, slammed me into the seat nearest the door, his skin gray and wet with perspiration.

"Murder," he said hoarsely, and wiped his face. "I've never tangled with murder before. Why did you do it, Sonia? Why did you do it? How did you expect to get away with murder, even with your looks? You may miss a first-degree rap but they'll send you up for long enough to spoil your looks for you."

"I didn't kill him. I didn't know him. I never saw him until today. And I'm not Sonia. I'm her cousin, Mary Quarles."

I didn't expect him to believe me but, considerably to my surprise and relief, he did. "Yeah," he said slowly, "with a murder charge facing her, Sonia wouldn't have clawed me up. She'd have clung like a leech." He squeezed into the seat across from me, which took a little maneuvering as he was a heavy man. "Who killed Kenyon?"

"I don't know. I was baby-sitting for the Millers next door. When I came back, Jack was here. Like that."

Brown fingered the heavy jowls where a dark beard was beginning to show. His hand was shaking. "Who's that guy who came around and tried to borrow my car? Said he was going for the police."

"Charles MacIntosh."

"Did he know about this?" He ducked his head toward Jack without taking his eyes off me.

"Yes."

"He's really gone for the police?"

"I don't know," I admitted miserably. "He's been

gone a long time. Mrs. Thomson wouldn't let him use her telephone. His tires have been slashed. The Batesons' car is drained of gas. My car keys have been stolen. When you wouldn't let him take your car, he said he'd have to walk until he found a telephone."

"Then we'd better get cracking. Let's have a look at it."

"At what?"

"No games. The necklace. And don't tell me you don't know about the necklace. That's why they sent you out here, to deliver it to me. And in case you doubt I'm the right man, I've got the cash on me. Cash, baby."

"I don't have the necklace."

"You mean you turned it over to this guy MacIntosh. What did he pay you for it?"

"I didn't."

He took my arm between thick muscular hands and began to twist it until I cried out. "I'm prepared to keep my share of the bargain. You keep yours and no tricks."

"It's gone," I gasped. "It's gone."

"What did you do with it?"

He dragged me to my feet and searched every inch of my body and then flung me across the trailer so that I landed on the couch, stumbling against Jack's shoulder as I pitched past him.

Brown pulled a small ugly gun out of his pocket. At least it was small enough to fit in his hand, but to me it looked like a cannon when he turned it on me.

"I keep this handy because of the stuff I carry with me. One false move out of you, sister, and you'll get it. Then the police are going to have two bodies to worry about."

He meant it. While he went over Jack's clothes and body, I sat huddled on the couch, my feet drawn up, eyes down so I would not have to watch his handling of that helpless body, that ultimate indignity. At last he jerked the body up and propped it against the couch. He yanked me down into the well beside him.

"What did you do with it?" His face was flushed and he was breathing hard.

"I don't know what happened to it. When I found Jack, the necklace was gone."

"I haven't time to search the whole damned trailer. But get this, sister. No one ever put anything over on me and got away with it."

My head snapped back as he slapped me across the face with his open hand. He slapped me again. He struck me with his fist, over and over. My eyes, my mouth, my nose, my jaw. Then he started on my body, hitting me again and again. I hadn't known it was possible to hurt so much.

Once a woman had described to me a terrible experience she had undergone during the Second World War when she had been captured and tortured by the Japanese for seventeen days. Only once in all that time had they wrested a scream from her.

"I wouldn't give them the satisfaction," she had told me grimly.

But mine is not the stuff of heroes. I screamed until I was hoarse but there was no one to hear me except the Batesons, and the noise from the Browns' television set probably drowned out my voice.

Then he kicked me on the shin, slipped in Jack's blood, lost his balance and fell, striking his head against the table support.

Almost before he landed I had opened the door. I ducked out of the light, began to run toward the Millers' trailer and realized that I must not lead Brown to Sam. A man of his caliber wasn't above using a child as a shield or as a threat. I swerved and raced on.

Because the empty trailer, which Paxton had told me was his, was dark, it seemed safer than Charles's lighted, wide-open one. I tried the door, which was unlocked, and went in, sagging against the wall, not knowing the arrangement of furniture, afraid to turn on lights, my breath coming in heavy gasps from running, the taste of blood from my nose warm and salty in my mouth. I tried to control my breathing so that I could hear Brown's approach. And near me something moved.

I held my breath and then, violently and uncontrollably, I sneezed.

"Mary?"

"Charles! What are you doing here in the dark? I thought you had gone for the police."

"Head bashed," he said in disgust. "I walked right into it. How long have I been out and how did you happen to look for me here?"

"I wasn't looking for you. I was running away from that man Brown." My voice was unexpectedly tart. Charles appeared to take for granted that my natural impulse would be to go looking for him.

I could hear him moving; he seemed to be on his hands and knees. Then he said disgustedly, "Give me a hand, will you? Every time I move my head I get dizzy."

I groped for him, helped him up, almost crying out with pain when he grasped one of my bruised arms. With our combined effort we got him onto a chair.

"Did you lock the door?"

"Yes."

"There's a light switch beside it, on the left. The curtains are drawn, so it will be all right. Now tell me about Brown. I warned you not to let anyone in. That guy is a wolf in wolf's clothing, and obviously on the prowl. I should think whistle-bait like you would have recognized the symptoms. I saw them, Mrs. Thomson saw them, Miller saw them, and so, if you remember, did Mrs. Brown."

I found the switch and the lights went on. Charles was sitting on a chair, his head resting against the back. He took one look at me and the change in his expression was almost ludicrous, if I had been capable, at that point, of being amused.

I must have been quite a sight. One eye was beginning to close. My nose was still bleeding and the blood had smeared on my face. My mouth was swollen and my lips were split. On my fair skin the marks of that terrible beating were already beginning to show up. By morning I'd be a sensational mass of color.

Charles came out of that chair as though he'd been fired from a gun. *"What did he do to you?"* I'd never heard that tone in a man's voice before but there was no mistaking it. This was a killer's voice.

"If you'll keep quiet, I'll tell you."

He got himself under control with an effort. "Go ahead."

I told him then. This wasn't easy, with his eyes fixed on me, because the one point that shrieked aloud, though I was careful not to utter it, was that I had left the trailer in the first place because I did not trust him.

That searching look of his unnerved me. He realized it and looked away.

"So Brown is the fence who disposed of Jack's stuff. I should have thought of that but I was so obsessed by the idea of the partner, I didn't wonder about how the stuff would be disposed of. Matter of fact, I suspected Sonia wouldn't let that much ice out of her greedy little cottonpickin' fingers. And when you couldn't produce the necklace, Brown did that to you."

He started for the door, aggressive in spite of the fact that he was weaving on his feet.

I didn't want any more violence. "Charles," I said, speaking as quietly as I could, "what I need is not a cave man but a lawyer."

He stopped short, took a long breath. "You're right, if I met Brown now I'd half-kill him and that wouldn't help the situation much." He put me in a chair, found towels, bathed my face gently and gave me a wet washcloth to hold on my nose to stop the

bleeding. This would have been easier if I hadn't continued to sneeze explosively.

The marks on my arms nearly set him off again.
There wasn't, he decided at length, anything broken,
though the place on my shin where Brown had kicked
me had a nasty gash. That was bleeding, too.

He rubbed my hair nearly dry with a towel. "Look
here, you are catching a terrific cold. You've simply
got to get out of that wet dress and into something
dry and warm. I have a change in my suitcase. Better
than nothing. Come over to my trailer."

After switching out the lights he opened the door
and listened. Then he caught my hand and we ran to
his trailer. In the bedroom at the back he pulled out
a suitcase. "Help yourself." The door closed behind
him.

I stripped off my clothes, toweled myself until I was
in a glow, though it hurt not only because I was so
bruised but because the sunburn had become real
agony. Then I put on Charles's slacks and sweater.
The slacks were both too long and too tight. The
length could be managed by turning them up at the
bottom; the tightness was beyond remedy. I pulled on
the sweater and, for the first time in hours, began to
feel warm.

When I got a good look at myself in the mirror, I
stopped worrying about whether or not the clothes
fitted me. Nothing on earth could have made me look
like anything except what I was—a battered wreck.

10

The house trailer was really like a house, surprisingly large, with two fair-sized bedrooms, a bathroom, kitchenette, and a roomy living room furnished with wicker chairs, tables, lamps, and a couch. From the standpoint of efficiency, it was probably a small miracle. From the standpoint of living, it was typical of a new element in the fabric of American life. A world of wheels instead of roots. A world of itinerant workers whose job kept them moving on, or of retired people searching restlessly for something they had never found. A world of strangers, meeting, passing, huddled together, yet eternally separate.

When I refused a drink, Charles set to work making coffee, talking quickly from the kitchenette. I had more or less collapsed on the couch, moving carefully because it hurt me, but at least my nose had stopped bleeding.

He had intended to try to get to a telephone, he explained, but the more he thought of it, the more uneasy he became at the idea of leaving me alone in the trailer park. If Paxton had killed Jack Kenyon—and he, for one, could see no alternative—he wasn't likely to go away, knowing that I could identify him. It would be too big a risk. He would hang around, waiting for a chance to get at me and, so far, he hadn't had that chance.

"So I tried to figure out where he might be hanging out while he waited for a clear field with you, and it struck me that the empty trailer he had claimed as his would be as good a place as any for a hideout. The door was unlocked; I walked in and he slugged me. Period."

"You really saw Paxton?" I exclaimed incredulously.

Charles put a cup of hot coffee in my hand. "Instant, but better than nothing and it will help warm you up. No, of course, I didn't see him."

"Oh." I was deflated. "Then you can't possibly be sure."

"I'm as sure as I need to be," he said shortly. "It's the only answer that makes any sense." He sat down, facing me, and I sipped cautiously at the scalding coffee.

"Are we just going to wait until the Millers come back before we get help?" I demanded.

He shrugged. "What else can we do? I'm damned if I am going to leave you alone here, particularly with Brown on the war path. Brown with a gun. A while ago, that's what you wanted me to do, wasn't it? To have me stay?"

"Yes, but—" I sipped coffee, thinking hard. Now and then I took a quick look at Charles. According to his story he had been slugged, knocked out, but I couldn't see a lump on his head. He looked all right. I wanted to believe him. Dear heaven, how I wanted to believe him!

"Suppose they meet," I said suddenly.

"Who?"

"That's what I heard Sonia saying to Jack. Suppose they meet."

Those colorless eyes of his studied me without appearing to see me. "Paxton and Brown. The partner and the fence. The necklace and the money. Damn it, there's really nothing to prevent the exchange, is there? Nothing to prevent Paxton from turning over the diamonds to Brown in exchange for the cash he told you he had." He set down his coffee cup. "No, we're just getting tangled up. The Kenyons would never sit back and risk having Paxton pocket the money from Brown. And if I am right, they lured Paxton here. He was to be killed and you, drunk again, were to be guilty, whether because you were defending your virtue or just being, in the revolting phrase, a mixed-up kid."

"Brown was expected. He was clear about that. He said he had been waiting all evening for me to make a move, to get in touch with him. As a matter of fact, I don't see why he wasn't just as likely to be the one who bashed you as Paxton. More likely."

"You mean, don't you, if someone did actually bash me." When I made no comment, Charles said pleasantly, "The possibility had occurred to you, hadn't it, that I was lying?"

I still could not think of an answer.

"You are wrong, of course, but I'd rather have liked you to believe in me without proof. Still, you can't have everything." His tone changed. "No, Mary, it wasn't Brown. They had been together all evening. And why Paxton has become such an object of solicitude to you, I can't imagine."

"He didn't act like a killer," I said stubbornly.

"You know, I've seen no indications that you know anything at all about people. You take them at their own valuation. Would you have guessed Brown was the kind of man who would beat you half to death?"

I shook my head.

"Let's not complicate things. The obvious explanation is that something went wrong with the Kenyons' plans. It's always possible that after they set up this trap for you and Paxton, they got word that Brown was coming for the necklace and it was too late to reach him and make any other arrangements."

"You're just guessing," I reminded him. "Oh, I wish the Millers would come soon, so that we could get help!"

There was a curious sound, a kind of enormous *puff,* and then the trailer was brilliant with light.

Charles jerked back the curtains from the picture window and I could see a sheet of flame.

"Good God! It's the gasoline outside the Batesons' trailer." A slow smile pulled his thin mouth thinner as he grinned. "So now we get help." The grin deepened. "Why couldn't I have thought of that myself?"

"Charles! Mr. Bateson has a bad heart."

The grin faded. "I'd forgotten." He opened the door, turned back. "You stay here."

I watched him run toward the Batesons' trailer wondering how he could make his way past that sheet of flame to help the elderly couple. Then I thought of Sam who was all alone. I don't remember now how I got there but I do remember the shaken relief when my groping hand found him, warm and safe and sleeping. For a moment I stood with my hand on the shoulder of the sleeping child and then I recalled Charles's warning.

I hated to awaken the little boy but I knew he'd be safer in Charles's trailer. We'd both be safer there. At least I hoped so. I wrapped him in a blanket and carried him out. Against the black sky the flames seemed incredibly bright. Dark silhouettes were running and women were shrieking in the panic caused by the suddenness of fire.

Sam stirred in my arms and awakened to roaring flames and hysterical screams. "Mother!"

"It's all right," I lied. "You're too big a boy to be afraid. Your mother is coming soon. Isn't that fire beautiful, Sam?"

He was much too sensible a child to be sidetracked by this idiotic red herring. "Mother," he wailed.

The door of the Batesons' trailer was opened. Outside, lighted by the roaring flames, were three people. The Seminole, who had been working on the grounds when I reached the trailer park, wasn't attempting to fight the gasoline fire but he was beating at the spreading brush fire with a broom. Mrs. Thomson was running back and forth, screaming and waving her hands.

Mrs. Brown, her handbag clasped to her rather capacious bosom, shouted, "Glenn! Glenn! Where are you? Come here."

I ran around them to Charles's trailer, locked the door, and sat down on the couch, rocking Sam in my arms, crooning foolish words to quiet him. If he got through this night without any lasting trauma, it would be a miracle.

Then someone kicked at the door and Charles called, "Mary, open up! Hurry!"

I set Sam down and ran to let him in. He was carrying Mr. Bateson. The old man's eyes were closed and his skin was the color of clay, curiously shrunken, the nose sharpened, the lips ominously blue. Sam forgot his own terror in his fascinated interest as Charles passed us to lay the old man gently on the bed in the back bedroom, kicking aside my wet dress, which I had dropped on the floor so it wouldn't stain the bed.

Mrs. Bateson followed them, pushed Charles aside, bent over her husband, a finger on his pulse. "May I have some water, please, and a spoon?"

She was completely under control. She took the glass Charles brought her, measured some drops carefully from the small bottle she had been clutching in her hand, directed Charles in lifting her husband's head while she got the medicine down without choking him.

When she looked up she even managed a smile. "Thank you. There's nothing more we can do now—except wait. If we could get him to a hospital, I'd like to have some things from our trailer but I don't know if it's possible."

"I'll see what I can do," Charles told her, "if you can give me a list of what you need."

She put out a restraining hand. "You took a big enough chance getting Bateson out of there. Don't try to go back. We're insured. Anyhow, human life is more important than things. At least that's what Bateson always says." For a moment her face crumpled and then she was steady again. "It was all so quick. I don't see what could have caused a fire like that. Right outside the trailer."

"That's one of the things we're going to find out," he promised her. He came back into the living room, noticed Sam, and realized for the first time that I must have disregarded his orders and left the trailer. By now, Sam was so engrossed in the proceedings that he was writhing like an eel in my arms, trying to watch what was going on outside and listening in fascination to that hysterical screaming.

For a moment Mrs. Bateson stood in the door of the bedroom, looking with startled eyes at the clothes I was wearing, at my battered face, at the little boy bouncing on my lap. Then her fleeting interest in anything but her husband faded and she closed the door, shutting us out.

"How serious is it?" I asked.

"If you mean Bateson," Charles said in a low voice, "it's quite bad, unless that medicine can fix him up. I wish to God we could get him to a hospital. Those damned screaming women and the fire—the combination is enough to give him another attack when—or if—he comes out of this one. But if you mean the fire, I doubt if it will spread unless a wind should come up. Thank heaven that breeze we had earlier has died down. The chief danger is a grass fire and the Indian is working hard to keep it down. The trailers are safe. I rather think this blaze will burn itself out. Mary, I beg you to listen to me. Don't do anything impulsive. You've got Sam now. There's no excuse for going out. Stay here. In all the confusion it would be so terribly easy for someone to get at you."

"Paxton or Brown?"

He said helplessly, "I don't know. But they can't either of them be far away. They must see this fire. They aren't trying to help. But that doesn't mean they are not around. Don't forget that. You're not very good at taking care of yourself, are you?" He took a long look at me, as though expecting the worst, and then went outside.

I heard him shouting, asking about fire equipment, heard the Indian reply that there wasn't any.

Then Mrs. Thomson ran screaming across the park. "You gotta help me get out my things! Fire caught that palm tree and it fell acrost the roof. Hurry!" I could see her claw at the Seminole.

Charles intervened. "Let him alone. He's doing the most important job. Did you call the fire department?

"No."

"Then the whole park will go and you won't collect a cent of insurance. If you fail to call the fire department, you are culpable—"

"No insurance?" she said hoarsely.

"Not a penny." He added impressively, "That's the law."

From his unrevealing face she could not determine whether he was telling the truth or not. She capitulated. "Awright, I'll call them." She ran toward the cottage. I could see some sparks flying. The fire was spreading over dry grass.

Charles and the Indian were working like an efficient team, beating out the sparks. Someone else was out there, too, screaming, impeding the work of the two men. Then Charles grabbed her and I realized that it was Mrs. Brown. He brought her into the trailer, pushed her down on a chair, and shoved a hand over her mouth.

"Shut up," he said savagely. "Mr. Bateson is in there. He has had a heart attack and he is in grave condition. Any extra excitement could kill him."

She pulled away his hand but she kept her voice low. "Where is Glenn? Where is my husband?"

"That," Charles told her grimly, "is what I'd like to know."

"We've got to find him." Cowed by his expression, she checked her rising voice. "We've got to get our things out of that trailer before the fire spreads any farther. I have three hundred dollars' worth of clothes in there."

"They're safer than they would be outside and I don't want you getting in the way. Don't worry, we'll find Brown. He did that to her." He nodded toward me. "He's going to pay for it if it's the last thing I ever do."

Mrs. Thomson came back at a shambling trot.

"Did you get them?" Charles asked her.

"I can't. The phone's outta order. I can't even raise a signal."

He shrugged. "That's that. Someone is bound to see the flames and call in a report." He caught up a small rug from inside the trailer and went out.

Mrs. Thomson tried to hold him back. "That's my rug. I could sue you for taking that."

"Do you want to save the rug or the park?"

"Okay, then. But how about my insurance? Would that cover the rug, too?"

"Get out of my way, for God's sake!"

She ran back to her cottage and came out with a small radio and lugging a portable television set. For a moment she stood holding them and then she set them down on the ground and went back inside. What possible purpose she thought she could be serving was beyond imagination but she was in a state of utter, unthinking panic.

Mrs. Brown was peering out of the window. "Looks to me like the whole place is going. Where is Glenn? Why doesn't he come back? What's he doing?"

"I don't know."

She turned to face me. "You must know where he is. What did you want with him?" For the first time she was aware of my change of clothing, of my battered face. "What was the idea of saying Glenn gave you that beating?"

"He did. He half-killed me."

"Serves you right," she said viciously. "You are Sonia Colette, aren't you? Always after other women's husbands. I saw a couple of your pictures. I don't know what you are up to, trying to pretend you are someone else and lying around in that bikini, trying to make every man in sight."

"I'm not Sonia." I blew my nose on Charles's handkerchief and it began to bleed again.

"No one would recognize you now," she said in a tone of satisfaction, "you little——"

"Sam is only four," I reminded her quietly.

"So what?" She gave me a queer look. For the first time I think she half-believed my story. "If you aren't Sonia Colette, who are you?"

"Her cousin."

"What did she have to do with Glenn? Is she an old flame of his?"

A car door slammed. There were raised voices and then Charles said something in a low tone. The Millers came in. Mrs. Miller saw nothing but her small son who beamed at her.

"It's a fire," he told her proudly.

They were both colorless with shock. Young Miller took Sam out of my arms and his wife touched the boy's cheek lightly with a shaking hand.

"Having fun?" she asked casually, and I gave her high marks.

"It's all burning up," Sam assured her. "Mary brought me over here where we could watch it."

Miller got his first real look at me. "My God! What happened to you?"

"I'll live"—I grinned at him—"but Mr. Bateson has had a heart attack——"

Charles came to the door, caught Miller's eye, and jerked his head. Miller put Sam in his wife's arms and went outside.

"For heaven's sake, where did you get those old pajamas, youngster?" Mrs. Miller asked.

I explained about his going out in search of Hotchkiss, though I was careful not to mention what had happened to the little dog, how he had gone into the

water, and I had had to find dry pajamas for him. I
was careful not to say that I had had to work on
him for several minutes before I could get air into his
lungs.

"I shouldn't have left him. I'll never forget you for
this, Mary Quarles."

"Just give me the first chance when you raffle him
off."

"What happened to you? Were you hurt when you
went in after Sam or in the fire?"

"Quite a lot has been happening around here," I
said evasively. With Sam wide awake and not missing
a word, I couldn't amplify. A murder. A stolen diamond necklace. The killing of a little dog. A terrible
beating. A fire. A heart attack. Two inexplicable dis-
appearances. Yes, quite a lot.

"How did the fire start? We saw the flames and
Tom must have had the car up to ninety, and on that
road! I imagined—" Her voice choked, her hands
tightened on Sam who wriggled and said, "You hurt."

Young Miller came back with Charles. There was
a queer look on the young man's face, so I gathered
that Charles had filled him in on at least some of the
highlights of the evening in the trailer park. The two
men went into the back bedroom. After a little while
they came out, Charles carrying the old man, Mrs.
Bateson behind them.

"Where are you going?" Mrs. Miller asked.

"We're taking Mr. Bateson to a hospital," her husband said. "We're going to call the fire department.
Bring the kid and come on, honey. You can sit in
back with Mrs. Bateson."

She tried to read his expression and gave up. "I
ought to get Sam a wrap, if it's safe to go back to our
trailer."

"Never mind the wrap. Get going," he said urgent-
ly. "Bring the kid the way he is. Hurry it up, honey."

There was no mistaking the urgency in his voice.
She clutched Sam tightly in her arms and followed

the little procession out of the trailer. I heard her ask her husband a question, heard her say, her voice high-pitched with surprise, "Police?"

"Police," Mrs. Brown repeated. "Everyone keeps saying that about police."

A car motor caught, throbbed; lights moved away toward the highway, then the red tail lights disappeared around a curve. Once more there was nothing but the sound of the fire, the thudding of running feet as Charles and the Seminole worked, and Mrs. Thomson's jittery excitement as she kept carrying things out of her cottage and stacking them on the ground outside, though there was more risk of their catching fire than if she had left them where they were. She had completely lost her head.

"What about Glenn?" Mrs. Brown said at last, speaking dully. "Has he gone off? Has he left me? Only how could he go? The car's still here."

"I don't know where he is. I ran away from him. He was still in the Scotty then."

"Why is everyone so determined to call the police?"

"There's a dead man in my trailer. He was stabbed. Murdered."

"Murder!" She wet her lips. "You meant it then about a body in the trailer. I thought it was just a come-on. Who is it?"

"His name was Jack Kenyon. He was my cousin's husband."

"Sonia Colette's husband? I remember their pictures after that secret marriage was revealed. He was the kind I could go for myself. What did he have to do with Glenn?"

"Mr. Brown knew him. He came here to the trailer park to meet Jack."

"I don't believe you. This was just a vacation."

"Mr. Brown told me so."

"So that's why, after promising me some fun at Miami Beach, he insisted on coming here. So we could be—alone, he said. Real private and no chance that anyone would recognize us." The pretense of marriage was gone in the face of murder. "God! Do you think Glenn did it?"

"No, I really don't. He was stunned when he saw the body and scared, too."

"Why did he want to meet this guy?"

"He wanted to buy a diamond necklace from Jack. He said he had the cash with him. He thought I'd taken the necklace myself or sold it to someone else. That's why he beat me."

"Glenn had cash on him to buy a diamond necklace!" After a long time, Mrs. Brown said, "I couldn't figure coming here to this dead joint. No fun or dancing or night clubs or anything to do. I thought the honest truth was that he was broke. He didn't even act—well, you know—interested in me. And the whole evening he seemed—I don't know how to explain it —kind of waiting for something. And all the time he had on him enough for a necklace. What was it worth?"

"I don't know diamonds. The other man, Paxton, said it must be worth a hundred thousand dollars."

She drew a long breath. "And that mink I wanted was going for only four hundred. Can you beat that?"

Her reaction to Jack's murder was almost as incredible as Mrs. Thomson's. I found myself gaping at her.

A siren rose and fell, swelled louder and louder; we saw the blinking red light coming into the park. The fire equipment had arrived.

There were voices and running feet, then another siren. A state police car pulled in behind the fire engine.

Charles appeared in the doorway, his face streaked with soot, dog weary but grinning.

"Okay," he said cheerfully, "the marines have landed."

11

The last spark had been extinguished and the fire engine had gone, but there was still a smell of burning in the air. Mrs. Thomson had made a frantic nuisance of herself all the time the firemen were working, trying to explain that she had attempted to call them but that her telephone was out of order. Would that affect her insurance?

Outside the big house trailer in which Mrs. Brown and I were still sitting, I could see a trooper talking to Mrs. Thomson, or, rather, listening to her. At length he broke off rather sharply to tell her to wait with the other ladies. She came in, glared at us, and sat down, listening as we were listening to what was being said outside.

"Who started this fire, anyhow?" the trooper asked Charles.

"Someone drained the gasoline from the Batesons' car and someone else, not knowing it was there, accidentally dropped a match in it. At least, that's the only explanation I can come up with."

"Who was having fun and games?" the trooper asked.

"It's worse than that. We've got a body here," Charles told him, and took him back to the Scotty.

It seemed to me that the three of us—Mrs. Thomson, Mrs. Brown, and I—sat waiting for hours. Actually, it was only a few minutes before Charles came into the trailer. There were two troopers with him.

One of them leaned against the door while the other sat down and pulled out a notebook.

"I am Sergeant Clay and this is Trooper Grant. We'll have to ask you some questions." He took a long, slow look from face to face. When he turned to me my heart sank. I knew what he saw, a battered and disreputable beatnik.

"Now then, you are the owner of this park, aren't you?"

Mrs. Thomson nodded vigorously. "Mrs. Thelma Thomson. And I've never had any trouble with the police. Nice people I get. Until she came here." A look stabbed in my direction.

"We'll come to that. Now let's get the names of all the people in this park, when they got here, all that. First trailer?"

"Most everyone come today. That first house trailer—and it's real nice, too—is the Browns'. This here is Mrs. Brown."

Clay looked at the woman who was twisting a handkerchief between her fingers, wrapping it around one of them like a bandage, straightening it out again.

"You are Mrs. Brown?"

"Mrs. Glenn Brown."

"Are you alone here?"

"No, my husband—" Her voice rose. "Where is my husband? Where is he? That girl came for him and he's never been back. Even when the fire started. Even when our trailer might have burned down. When I might have been hurt. Where is he?"

Clay held up a hand to check her. "Your address?"

For a moment Mrs. Brown stared at him, mouth half-open. "Well—"

"They'll check, you know," Charles broke in to tell her. "You might as well tell the truth now. It's bound to come out."

The handkerchief ripped as she tugged at it. "All right," she said sullenly, "so we aren't married. I'm Mrs. Anthony Mercer from Minneapolis. Glenn—we met at a nightclub out there and got along fine, and all my husband likes is to go hunting and fishing. Fishing! I ask you. So we thought we'd take a little jaunt. Miami Beach, he said. I told my husband that my aunt was going to have an operation and I had to be with her. We're of age."

"Sure. Sure." The sergeant made a note while color crept over the woman's face in an ugly tide.

"Do you have to tell my husband about this?" she asked painfully.

"Well, now, I can't promise, you know. We'll see when the time comes. Depends a lot on what you— on what Mr. Brown has been up to."

"I don't know where he is. That girl came for him and he went out after her like a bat out of hell. And I haven't laid eyes on him since. Not even when the fire broke out. He never even came back to see if I was all right."

"What's his business?"

"He's a salesman. Insurance."

"What company?"

"He—I don't know. Look, Sergeant, you understand how these things happen. Perfectly natural and no harm done to anyone. I didn't have a thing to do with all this. I don't know a thing. Does my name have to get in the paper? That's what I'm asking you."

"I don't know yet. Next?" Clay said to Mrs. Thomson.

"The second trailer. That's this one. MacIntosh rents it. He come today, like the rest of them. Except her."

The evil old eyes rested on my battered face. It was the first time she had really taken a good look at me since my beating. Her lips parted in astonishment and then shaped themselves in a grin of pure pleasure.

"Quite a coincidence, everyone coming at once. The park has been empty since last fall, hasn't it?"

"I hadn't got around to fixing it up," Mrs. Thomson muttered uneasily.

Clay's eyebrows shot up. "You haven't been renting these house trailers?"

"No, I—" She saw his expression, broke off. "People come by for a night, now and then," she mumbled. "Travelers who don't want to go any farther. And that's what trailer parks are for, isn't it? No harm in that. We could make some arrangement, I suppose."

It wasn't her own corruption that took me aback; it was her serene assumption that everyone is corrupt. I half-expected Clay to blast her clear to kingdom come, but he made no reply, simply jotted down another note. Then he looked at Charles, who pulled identification out of his wallet.

"San Francisco. You've come a long way. Occupation?"

"I'm an attorney. And I came here on business for a client."

"To this particular trailer park, you mean?"

"Yes."

"Client's name?"

"Privileged," Charles reminded him.

For a moment the two men studied each other and then the sergeant said without emphasis, "We'll come back to that." He had a pleasant voice and a pleasant manner, not at all the kind of man who throws his weight around when he wears a uniform. But not the kind of man, either, to stand for any nonsense.

He turned to Mrs. Thomson. "Next?"

"That third house trailer is unoccupied," she said.

At the same time I said, "That's where Paxton was staying."

"There isn't any such man. Never was," Mrs. Thomson insisted. "No one is renting that trailer. Hasn't since last fall. I keep telling you."

"Someone was in there not long before the fire," Charles said. "He knocked me out."

The sergeant's eyes went from one face to the other like a ping-pong ball. "Next?"

"The Batesons," Mrs. Thomson told him. "Old retired couple who come in today. He was worn out from driving, not used to hauling a trailer, and they couldn't get any farther. The fire broke out right beside their trailer and he had a heart attack. The next travel trailer is the Millers', a young couple with a small boy. They liked this place, right on the gulf and all. Good for the kid. They plan to stay for a week or so. They're the ones who took Bateson to the hospital. They aren't back yet."

The sergeant nodded. "They also called the fire department and us. Well, we know where they are. The sheriff's office will keep an eye on them for the night."

"It's ridiculous to think they had anything to do with this," I said. "They went into town before Jack was killed and they've been gone all evening."

Sergeant Clay looked me over. He didn't miss a thing—from those preposterous and ill-fitting clothes that belonged to Charles to my swollen nose, puffy eyes, cracked lips, the lump on the side of my jaw. I'd pinned my hair up in a knot to keep the damn strands from falling into my eyes.

"Your name?"

"Mary Quarles." I sneezed violently. At least my nose didn't start bleeding again. Automatically, as though it were already an accustomed old habit, Charles thrust a clean handkerchief into my hand.

"Address?"

"Lloydsville, New York."

"Did you arrive today, too?"

I nodded. "Late afternoon."

"That your Scotty?"

"No, it belongs to—" I swallowed. "It belonged to Jack Kenyon. He's the one who is in there, the one who was murdered."

"It is so her trailer," Mrs. Thomson put in. "Mr. Kenyon told me. He was keeping an eye on her. She's been out here, drunk and disorderly, carrying on and making scenes, for the most of three days, and he kept looking in to see she didn't do herself any harm. And then she kilt him."

Charles and I both started to speak at the same time. Clay put up his hand, rather like a schoolteacher controlling an obstreperous class.

"Jack Kenyon? Actor doing a show at the hotel, isn't he?"

"Yes, he was an actor. A night-club singer, really. He was married to my cousin, Sonia Colette."

He looked up alertly, as most men did at the mention of Sonia. "Just tell me in your own words what happened, Mrs.—uh—"

"It's Miss Quarles. Where do I start?"

"Why did you come out here?"

I began with Sonia's long-distance telephone call, asking me to visit her in Florida, explained how I had driven down and learned from her that there were no available rooms at the Kenyons' hotel and, in fact, no place in town where I could stay overnight. Clay gave me a quick look, started to speak, made a brief note. I knew then that he didn't believe me.

"So I came on here for the night. Apparently it was the only thing to do. I didn't plan to stay more than one night. They had just got another engagement, in Arizona, I think, so I intended to go back to New York tomorrow. I—I didn't like it here."

"Nice place I got," Mrs. Thomson said. "Nice people." Her eyes stabbed at me. "Until she came."

"It didn't occur to you to try to find a place you liked better?" Clay asked me smoothly.

"Well, I couldn't. Jack had forgotten to cash a check and he took all my money to tide him over. I haven't anything but seventy-five cents. And, anyhow, my car keys are missing. I was just—stuck."

Charles put in quickly, "I had better explain, Sergeant, that with the exception of the Browns' car, all of them are out of commission. That's what caused the delay in calling you when the murder was discovered, and later in getting the fire department when the blaze broke out. My car has the tires slashed. The Batesons' was drained of gasoline."

"No telephone?"

"Someone put mine out of order," Mrs. Thomson said hoarsely. "I tried to call the fire department. Honest to God. Does that hurt my insurance?"

Clay blinked at her in some surprise. All he said was, "Telephone out of order." He made a note. "Now this Jack Kenyon," he went on without a pause. "You knew him well, Mrs. Thomson?"

"Not to say well. But he brought that girl out the day he hauled in her Scotty and he paid a week in advance. Trying to get her in some sort of shape and sobered up. For his wife's sake, he said."

"When did you see him last?"

"Somewheres around three o'clock this afternoon. I'd been busy, what with two people coming in to rent house trailers, and then those two travel trailers to be connected up and all."

"Go on."

"Well, he was just as nice as ever, and that good-looking! He was surprised to see I'd got some people because the Scotty had been the only one that was occupied when he was out yesterday. He opened it up and got the fan going so's it would be cool when that girl come back. She'd run into town with him the night before. He left a bottle of bourbon for her and said for her to have fun."

Once more Clay's cool appraising eyes took in every mark on my face. If he thought I'd got in that condition while in a drunken frenzy, who was to blame him? He only said again, "Go on."

"Well, that's the last time I ever saw him. Alive, that is. Next time was when he"—and she looked at Charles—"come over to use my telephone. Said he had to call the police because there was a dead man in the Scotty. I didn't believe him, so I went to see for myself." She swallowed.

"Now, Miss Quarles," the sergeant said. Charles started to intervene, but he held up his hand. "Later. Later. Well, Miss Quarles?"

"Tell them the truth, Mary," Charles said.

I know that he meant to be helpful but the effect was dubious, to say the least. I told the sergeant about the discovery that my car keys were missing. I'd gone in swimming and had fallen asleep on the sand. When I got back to the trailer, I knew that someone had been in it during my absence.

"How?"

"Sonia's bathing bag was on the floor in the well of the trailer. I'd put it on the couch. I'm sure of that. I'm rather an orderly person." Seeing his eyes sweep over me, I could feel hot blood burning in my cheeks.

"Go on."

"Then Charles—Mr. MacIntosh came."

"You've known him long?"

"Just—since this afternoon."

"I see." What he could see was obvious.

"He went there, all right," Mrs. Thomson put in viciously. "I just happened to drop by, wanted to know if she had found those car keys she was making such a stew about, and there he was. His arm around her. I said, right then and there, I wouldn't have goings-on in this trailer park. I never have. I never will."

Something in Clay's expression gave me the first small stirring of comfort. I thought he was shrewdly aware that the lady did protest too much.

"Why didn't you tell the sergeant why I was in Miss Quarles's trailer, that I'd taken her some sunburn lotion because she was badly burned, that Mrs. Bateson had urged her to do something about it?" Charles was glaring at Mrs. Thomson. It occurred to me that he was very angry indeed, in spite of the studiously detached manner he had maintained so far.

Mrs. Thomson's loose mouth twisted derisively.

"That's what he told me, Sergeant," she said jocularly. "Sure as anything, that's what he told me."

"And then?"

I looked at Charles, looked away again. "And then Char—Mr. MacIntosh asked me to give it to him. He said he wouldn't go away until I did." I gave Charles a quick look, but he was smiling.

"Give him what?"

"I thought he meant the letter but he meant the necklace."

The sergeant leaned back in his chair, looking from me to Charles. For a moment I thought he was going to break out in irritation, but he was a doggedly patient man. "Let's get this straight," he said mildly.

I told him about the envelope Sonia had given me. She had said someone would come to the trailer for it, that it was desperately important, that she was in an awful jam.

"She didn't explain what this—jam was all about?"

I shook my head.

"Have you got the envelope?"

"No, I gave it to him."

Charles pulled the envelope out of his pocket and handed it to the sergeant. "Nothing in it but a piece of blank paper."

For the first time the sergeant's mouth tightened. "You people trying to give me the runaround?" he asked suspiciously.

"No, we aren't. Honestly. I think the letter was just Sonia's excuse for getting me out here. What Charles really wanted was the necklace." As Clay looked blank, I added earnestly, "The diamond necklace I found in the icebox drain."

In the sergeant's wary expression I saw the first inkling that he thought I was either drunk or mad or, more likely, both. In a way, I didn't blame him.

"Do you have the necklace, too, Mr. MacIntosh?" he said dryly.

"No, I think Paxton stole it when he killed Kenyon. Probably Brown has it now."

Clay ran his fingers through his hair, they dug into his scalp as though he were trying to keep a firm hold on his sanity.

"There isn't any Paxton," Mrs. Thomson cried. "I keep telling you that. No one named Paxton in this place. That girl kilt Mr. Kenyon. She kilt him."

"That," Charles said, "is what everyone was meant to think. This whole deal was set up for Mary. Only it backfired. The wrong man was murdered."

"Suppose"—the sergeant raised his voice—"you let me handle this in my own way." He was a trifle punch-drunk but still functioning gamely. "When was Kenyon killed? Who found him?"

"I found him." My voice was shaking and I swallowed hard before I went on. The man Paxton—and I looked defiantly at Mrs. Thomson—had dropped by, and helped me to fix the gas stove, and I'd told him he could stay to dinner.

"Every man in sight," Mrs. Mercer muttered to her clenched hands. "Glenn and MacIntosh and every man in sight."

"I asked him," I said, steadying my voice, "because I was afraid of Charles." Again I looked at him, again he smiled reassuringly. "I thought Charles was the man Sonia was afraid of. I wanted someone with me in case he came back."

I explained how, in trying to fix the leak in the ice-box, I had found the necklace. "Mr. Paxton said the diamonds must be worth at least a hundred thousand dollars. So then—"

"Go on."

"I thought there was a prowler. I kept hearing sounds as though someone was moving around outside the trailer."

"So did I," Mrs. Brown—or Mrs. Mercer—said unexpectedly. "I kept telling Glenn. I heard it, too. That is why I tried to get him to leave, but he insisted on

hanging around. I've never been in a place like this
before, so desolate, away from anything and anybody.
If there was a prowler, he'd be up to no good. I was
scared, I can tell you."

"No prowlers around here," Mrs. Thomson said
firmly. "Nice people I get." The phrase was like an
incantation in which she devoutly believed.

"Go on," Clay said rather wearily.

"So," I said, "then the little dog, Hotchkiss, began
to bark." I had to go back at this point and explain
about the little mongrel dog that Sam had found and
that Mrs. Thomson had not allowed him to keep in
the park. "The dog's barking wakened Sam and he began to call." Again I backtracked to say I'd offered to
baby-sit while the Millers went into town for the evening. So I had gone over to the Millers' trailer—

"Leaving a strange man alone with a diamond necklace." There was no expression on the sergeant's nice
face.

"I had to. As it was, Sam had waded out into the
water—the tide was coming in—he went down and I
had a bad time finding him. That's why"—I indicated
Charles's clothes—"I had to put these on. I didn't have
anything else and I was catching cold."

"Just for the record," Charles said evenly, "I may
point out that Miss Quarles twice saved the little boy's
life today and that a child's safety was more important
to her than a diamond necklace."

The sergeant did not seem to hear him. "Go on,
Miss Quarles."

"I found—" I swallowed and then told him about
finding the little dog. "It was dead. Its skull had been
beaten in." I broke off again. "They needn't have
killed the dog! They didn't have to do that!"

Clay looked at the trooper who had been lounging
against the door and the latter went out.

"Well, then," I went on when my voice was steady,
"I got Sam out. He'd swallowed a lot of water and it
took a while to bring him around; then I had to dry

him off and find fresh pajamas; and then—I hated to leave him. He was so small and he had been frightened and nearly drowned and his mother wasn't there. So I told him stories until he fell asleep."

"How long did all this take?"

"Perhaps half an hour in all. Surely not more than that. So then I went back." My heart began to race and I was breathless. I tried to breathe deeply, to speak slowly. "The Scotty was dark. I slipped in something—wet."

My hands were damp and I wiped them on Charles's handkerchief. "I stumbled over something and thought it was Sonia's bathing bag again. I bent down and felt—and turned on the light. And he was there, crumpled up on his face, and the steak knife was between his shoulders."

"Okay, Mary." Charles reached forward, put his hand over mine. "Okay, take it easy."

Sergeant Clay apparently realized that I couldn't say any more at the moment.

"Well, Mr. MacIntosh?"

Charles hesitated so long that my heart went cold. Again ugly distrust stirred in me. When he finally spoke he said cautiously, "As I told you, I came here in the interests of a client. I'll have to withhold my client's identity at this time; in fact, until I have permission to use it. I'll tell you as much as I can of what I know about this. My mission was to recover, without scandal or publicity, a diamond necklace she believed had been stolen from her by Jack Kenyon. I traced him and the trailer to this park. Mistaking Miss Quarles for her cousin—"

At this, the sergeant gave him a look of wonder, as though suspecting his brain had become unhinged.

"I went to demand the return of the necklace. She thought I meant the letter her cousin had given her, and handed it to me. When I opened it I didn't know what the hell sort of game she was playing. Later I came back and found her staring down at the dead man. She had assumed, because she could not see his face, that it was Paxton whom she had left in the trailer. We looked at him and she identified him as Jack Kenyon, her cousin's husband."

"You thought the murdered man was Paxton, the man whom no one but you has ever seen." The sergeant's eyes rested idly on the lump on my jaw, on my swollen mouth. He turned to Charles. "But it turned out to be the man whom you had come to see, the man from whom you intended to retrieve a necklace."

"I hadn't expected Kenyon." Charles spoke quickly. "I simply assumed the necklace must be hidden somewhere in the trailer. Kenyon wouldn't have risked carrying it around with him. I intended to recover it."

"And then Kenyon appeared on the scene."

"I never saw Kenyon until after he was dead. And I didn't kill him, Sergeant. A lawyer does what he can for his clients but murder's beyond the call of duty."

Clay studied him for a moment. The eyes of the two men met, held.

"We'll come back to that. Make no mistake about it, MacIntosh"—no "Mr." now—"we'll come back to it. So what happened after you discovered the dead man was Jack Kenyon?"

"I headed for Mrs. Thomson's cottage at once to use her telephone and call the police."

But it hadn't, I remembered, been like that. He had stayed in the Scotty with me half an hour—three-quarters of an hour. Probably even more.

"Very commendable of you," Clay said blandly. "And you found the telephone out of order, of course."

He doesn't believe either of us, I thought.

"I don't know," Charles said, "whether it was out of order then or not. At that time Mrs. Thomson refused to let me use it. She said she didn't believe me. She went back to the Scotty with me and saw for herself. She was panic-stricken. Her idea was that we would drag the body out of the trailer and hide it, or dispose of it, somehow, so that the park wouldn't be involved in any publicity. In fact, she put up a fight, grabbed his arm, tried to haul him out herself."

"Did she now?" the sergeant murmured.

"That's a lie! That's a lie! The girl and he are both lying."

The trooper named Grant came back. "I found the dog, all right. The skull has been crushed."

The two men looked at each other in silence. Then once more Grant settled himself against the door.

Clay turned to Charles. "So what did you do when you couldn't use the telephone?"

"I tried to start my car and discovered that all the cars, with the exception of Brown's, were out of commission."

"With the exception of Brown's." The sergeant looked at the young trooper who went out again. "And the Browns wouldn't let you use their car, even to report a murder?"

"Look," Mrs. Mercer said desperately, "you've got to see it my way. All right, I was a fool to come off with Glenn for a couple of weeks, but it's not as though people don't do it all the time. It's not as though we weren't old enough to know our own minds. After the dull life I lead, I thought I owed it to myself to have some fun. And Glenn said he had to make this Florida trip, all of a sudden, and I thought we'd have some fun at Miami Beach. And, instead, he came here and rented that crummy house trailer."

Mrs. Thomson stiffened but, at a peremptory gesture from Clay, she was silent.

"I thought at first Glenn was just broke and then I thought—well, you know how it is—that the joke was on me. But he was kind of uneasy, on edge, and there was the prowler."

"You're sure about the prowler?"

"If you mean did I see him, no. But you could hear footsteps in the sand, and a grating sound when he stepped on a shell, and blundering around like. Maybe that was when he was fixing the cars."

"But why not Mr. Brown's car?"

"I think the prowler must have been Jack," I said suddenly.

"And why would he have been hanging around here for hours?" Clay asked.

"Because," Charles said, "he was waiting for Paxton to show, and Paxton was mighty careful to keep out of sight until he knew what the score was."

"And," I added, "Jack wouldn't want Mr. Brown's car out of order because Mr. Brown was going to buy that necklace. Mr. Brown told me so himself. He thought I'd sold it to Charles. That's why he half-killed me. He struck me and struck me. Then he kicked me and lost his balance and slipped in Jack's blood——" I gulped. "And I ran away from him. I ran to Paxton's trailer because it was dark and I thought it would be safe. And Charles was there. He had been knocked out."

"MacIntosh was there," Clay said in a thoughtful tone. "You seem to have made a remarkable recovery from a blow that knocked you out."

"It's true, just the same," Charles told him.

"So we have one missing diamond necklace and two missing men." Again Clay dug his fingers into his scalp as though trying to control the confusion there. "And where the sweet hell are they?"

Heavy footsteps pounded across the sand, the door of the trailer opened and the young trooper said, "Hey, for God's sake, Sergeant, we've got another body!"

12

"No one," the sergeant said, "is to leave this trailer without permission. Is that clear?" He looked from face to face and then went out with the trooper.

For a moment we sat in stunned silence. Beyond the Browns' trailer we could hear the voices of the two men, could see flashlights. The younger trooper ran back to the official car to use the radio telephone.

It was Mrs. Thomson who broke the silence in her inimitable manner. "This is going to give my park a bad name. I'll sue someone for this."

"My God," Mrs. Mercer said, almost in a whisper, "this will hit every paper in the country. Names and everything."

I had thought that the night had made me almost shockproof, but the self-centeredness of those two women continued to rock me. Neither of them had so much as wondered whose body had been found, how he had died, who had killed him.

Charles put his arm around me and I leaned back against his shoulder, comforted and fortified.

Sergeant Clay was back again, a very grim Sergeant Clay. Up to now he had given us all a lot of rope, I realized that. From now on we were in real trouble.

"MacIntosh?"

Charles's arm tightened around me for a moment and then he got up and followed the sergeant. It was some time before he returned.

"Mrs. Thomson?" Clay said.

When she had gone with him, silenced for once, I whispered to Charles, "Who is it?"

"Later." He held my hand so hard he hurt me. There was no more detachment in his face. "All hell has broken loose."

Apparently Mrs. Thomson had been ordered to return to her cottage, because the sergeant came back alone.

"Mrs. Mercer?"

"Is it Glenn?"

"That's what I want you to tell me."

She got up and stumbled toward the door. Clay took her arm, supporting her as they walked back to Brown's car.

"Was it Brown?" I asked.

Grant had returned. He looked white and excited. "No talking, please."

I heard Mrs. Brown scream once and then she broke into hysterical sobbing. They were coming back. Apparently the sergeant was trying to control her, to get her into the trailer Brown had rented, but she broke away from him, ran to the open door of the trailer in which we were sitting, shoving the trooper to one side.

"You killed him! You killed him!" With her arm outstretched, she pointed an accusing finger at Charles like something out of an amateur production of *Medea*. "You said you'd make him pay for what he did to the girl, beating her up. You said so."

The sergeant nodded to Grant who dragged her away, still shouting accusations.

"Miss Quarles."

"I represent Miss Quarles," Charles intervened.

"You practice law in Florida?"

"She has a right to legal advice."

"Her rights will be protected. Miss Quarles, will you come with me, please." It was courteously phrased but it was an order, not a request.

"Mary——"

"It's all right, Charles." I followed the sergeant to the Browns' house trailer where the television set incongruously began to blare. Beyond the trailer there was a big black Buick. The left front door was open and Brown was hunched over, his face resting on the wheel. Whoever had killed him had battered his head savagely, a piece of bone showed where the scalp had been lacerated. Jack's murder, the gleaming steak knife in his back, had been horrible enough. But this was nightmare. The bone wasn't stark and clean; it was filthily messy.

I found myself clutching at Clay's arm. He never took his eyes off my face. With his free hand he leaned forward to raise that mangled head.

"Don't," I choked.

"Take a look at him."

I bent over, so close that my cheek brushed against the dead arm, and peered into his face. It was scratched as though a cat had clawed at it, scratches on which the blood had dried.

"Did you make those scratches?"

"Yes," I said numbly. "Yes. He tried to kiss me, he was being offensive. I scratched him and he let me go. But I didn't—you can't kill anyone by scratching them. And anyhow I couldn't—he was armed. He had a gun."

"Took you a long time to remember that, didn't it? What kind of gun?"

"I don't know firearms. It was small." I demonstrated with my hands. "He threatened me with it when I said I didn't have the necklace. But he wasn't —shot."

"As you see. No, Miss Quarles, he was clubbed to death."

"He was alive when I ran away from him, Sergeant. He—wait. I told you he lost his balance and fell, striking against the table support. Maybe that——"

"And then he got up, walked across the park to his

car and got in under his own steam. Or perhaps you think he hit himself over the head hard enough to smash his own skull."

"I don't know what happened to him but he was alive. I swear he was alive. I didn't know he was even hurt; I thought he was just off balance, that he'd follow me. That's why I didn't dare go to the Millers' trailer, though it was the nearest. A man like that—and a little child—"

"How much money was he carrying?"

"He didn't tell me. Just that he had the money. He said, 'Cash, baby.' "

"You have no money, Brown has no money. Someone must be carrying quite a wad right now."

"And the necklace," I reminded him.

"Yes, that diamond necklace. How long have you known MacIntosh?"

"We've both told you, over and over. I never saw him until I came here this afternoon. Can we please—must we stay here any longer?"

"Does it bother you? You must have been real mad after that beating Brown gave you. MacIntosh didn't like it either, did he?" He raised his voice in sudden whiplash irritation. "For God's sake, shut off that television set." Grant went running, forced Mrs. Brown to open the door of the trailer to which she had returned. After he had spoken forcibly, she switched off the set. Then there was blessed quiet. Once more the rhythmic beat of the tide filled the night.

As I stared toward Charles's trailer, the sergeant halted me, his hand on my arm. "There's no hurry to get back, Miss Quarles. Suppose you tell me just what you did when you went to that empty trailer next door. After you had run away, leaving Brown alive."

"But I didn't do anything. I went there because it was dark and closed up and seemed safer, less exposed than Charles's, where the door and windows were open and the lights were on. And I found Charles there. He had been knocked out."

"Would you swear under oath that he was unconscious when you found him?"

"No, but he was still groggy. He was down on the floor and he couldn't get up without my help."

"He seems pretty lively now. Odd way to be looking for the police, don't you think? An empty trailer?"

"He was looking for Paxton. He was afraid he was still hanging around."

"Why?"

"Because, if Paxton had killed Jack, I was the only one who had seen him and who could identify him. Charles didn't want to leave me alone. He thought I was in danger. And we knew the Millers would be home before long, that they could get the police."

"Tell me again about this prowler of yours."

Again I told him as well as I could, though there was really nothing to say except that I had heard movements, muffled sounds. Paxton had heard them, too; he had kept warning me there was a prowler; he had said that was why he had really come to the trailer, to make sure I was all right. And Hotchkiss had heard him, and then he stopped barking when he was killed.

"Now I missed that before," Clay said alertly. "You mean this man Paxton was with you when the dog was killed."

I nodded.

"So the prowler must have been Brown or MacIntosh."

"It couldn't have been Brown because his wife—his —Mrs. Mercer said he was with her until he came to my trailer. And anyhow she heard the prowler while Mr. Brown was with her."

"And that leaves MacIntosh," Clay said in a tone of satisfaction.

"Don't you see, Sergeant, the prowler must have been Jack Kenyon."

"And Kenyon's spirit trailed MacIntosh to a trailer

and clipped him one some time after he was dead."

"No, that must have been Paxton. But earlier——"

"According to what you said first, Kenyon sent you out here, knowing the necklace was in the trailer, knowing Brown was coming. Seems peculiar, doesn't it?"

"Charles thinks it was an attempt to frame me." I told him the whole story then: Sonia impersonating me at the trailer park, her sending me there in the dress and bikini and distinctive dark glasses she had worn on the beach.

"And what was all this supposed to be in aid of?"

"Charles thinks Paxton was a former business partner of Jack's, that he kept the necklace instead of sharing the proceeds with him, that he intended to kill him because Paxton could expose his activities and ruin his career, that he intended to set me up as the killer but that I, too, was to die. An overdose of drugs."

"Sorry," Clay said at last. "I'm just not buying it. I could think of half a dozen more plausible explanations for those two murders without half trying. But, of course, they wouldn't be apt to clear your friend MacIntosh so neatly."

He turned his flashlight on a dark object on the ground beside the Buick, a heavy hammer with its head smeared with blood and something else. With his eyes on my face he said, "Same weapon that killed the little dog. Not a nice character to run up against."

"No," I agreed.

"MacIntosh has a way of protecting your interests." He didn't make it sound protective; I don't think he meant to.

"Where are we going?"

"Back to the Scotty. We're going through the whole story again."

Outside the door of Jack's trailer my feet stopped of their own accord. I couldn't go in there again.

"Okay," Clay said, "Come on and let's get it over."

He unlocked the door and I went in because I had no choice.

"Now then." He took me, almost minute by minute, from my arrival at the park to my discovery of Jack's murder. He pounded at me about Paxton, the man whom nobody else had seen. He jumped to the fire, which had started in the pool of gasoline outside the Batesons' trailer. By that time I was snatching wildly at any point even remotely in my favor.

"Charles and I were together in his trailer when the fire started. Don't you see that someone else must have been there to set it?"

Before I could tell whether my point had registered, he took me through that ugly interview with Brown.

"He thought you were your cousin?"

"Yes. At first. Then he believed me."

"But not about the necklace."

"Not about the necklace. He thought I had either kept it for myself or sold it to Charles. He said no one ever put anything over on him and got away with it."

"He seems to have been wrong about that, doesn't he?" When I made no comment, he said, "Now when you went to the Browns' trailer—for help, I think you told me—"

"For help."

It went on and on, his quiet voice never threatening, just inexorable.

At last he took me out of the trailer, locked the door.

"Are you going to arrest me?"

"We'll have to hold you as a material witness until we get the answers to a lot of questions, Miss Quarles."

"I've told you every single thing I know about this, over and over again."

"Maybe you'll think of something more. People often do when they have plenty of time to think. And you'll have plenty of time to think. Coming, Miss Quarles?"

Not, of course, that there was any choice. As we started back across the trailer park we heard Mrs. Thomson shouting.

"That woman ought to be muzzled," the sergeant muttered. "What's the difficulty now?" he called.

"The Seminole who works for me," the manager explained. "Never around when I want him. I need him to get my things back in the cottage. He helped real good with the fire but now he's run off somewheres."

"Where does he live?"

"That shack back of the trailer park. I let him have it and his keep and fifteen dollars a week."

The Seminole, a short stocky fellow, oily black hair held in place by a red band tied around his forehead, came into the pool of light outside Mrs. Thomson's cottage. He was not alone. The man he was leading—I blinked in astonishment—was young Paxton.

"Found him under a tree back of my place. He'd been knocked out," the Indian said.

Paxton's mouth was white, a thin line of pain. One eye was almost closed and his cheek was grazed and discolored. The cuffs of his trousers were scorched.

I realized now that the Indian was not propelling Paxton. The latter was hanging on to him. He looked around, dazed, seeing the evidence of the fire, the troopers, me.

"Miss Quarles!" he exclaimed. "Good God, you've been hurt. What happened to you?"

As he swayed, Clay caught him, helped him into Charles's trailer, and the rest of us crowded after, with Mrs. Thomson bringing up the rear. In a moment Mrs. Mercer came running to join us.

"Who is this?" Clay asked.

"That is Mr. Paxton," I said, with a look of triumph at Mrs. Thomson.

The sergeant eased Paxton into a chair and Charles offered to make more coffee for everyone. While we waited for the water to boil, Clay turned to the Indian.

Before he could question him, I caught sight of the man's hands, covered with deep burns. I made him show them to me, ordered Mrs. Thomson to her cottage for First Aid cream and bandages. She was so surprised that she went off at a trot. Clay made no attempt to intervene while I squeezed the cream thickly over the burns and bandaged those blistered hands.

"It must hurt horribly." I was furious. He had worked like mad to help fight the fire and then no one had even wondered about him, let alone thanked him. When the bandages were in place, his hands looked bulky and awkward. "Only a few minutes," I assured him, "and you'll feel better. Charles, give the man a good stiff drink."

Without comment, but with a lurking amusement in his eyes, Charles poured a drink. The Indian couldn't manage the glass with his painful hands, so I held it to his lips, tipping it slowly until he had swallowed it all.

"Now," Clay began patiently.

In answer to his questions the Indian went through the day. It had not been a usual day. No one had been around all week except for the girl in the little Scotty. There hadn't been much to do since the hurricane except for cleaning up after parties two or three times a week. People from town came out to rent the house trailers and, usually, if the party was rough, as it generally was, they left things in a mess.

Mrs. Thomson's loose mouth writhed with fury but a look from the sergeant kept her silent.

But today had been different, the Indian went on. People had come to rent house trailers and some new people with travel trailers came in—an old couple beat up from traveling, a young couple who wanted to keep their sick kid out in the sunshine. And this afternoon the girl had come back, this time alone and driving a little Renault. Before that she had come in a Ford driven by the actor fellow.

So there had been a lot to do, parking the travel

trailers, connecting them up. He had had his supper at his own place and then had gone to bed, but he couldn't sleep. A television set was making such a racket it's a wonder they hadn't heard it in town— shots, screams, all the works. Then a mongrel dog the kid had picked up on the beach barked its head off.

"What at?" Clay asked casually.

"There was someone around," the Indian said. "A couple of times I went out to see who it was. We never had no prowler before. I didn't see no one, but I knew someone was there. I kind of felt him, the way you do."

He had just been dropping off to sleep when the fire started. Then that guy—a nod at Charles—took a big chance and got the old man and his wife out of their trailer and brought them over here. The old man looked like he was dying. Then the girl had run like a wild woman, a wonder she hadn't gone right through the flames, to get the little boy and bring him back here. He and that guy had done their best to put out the fire but it was gasoline. You could tell. About all they could do was to try to keep it from spreading.

The fire equipment had come at last and the fire was put under control. When it was over he decided to get some sleep if he could, what with his hands hurting that way. Mrs. Thomson had hauled all that stuff outside her cottage and she'd expect him to drag it back for her. So, he figured, instead of sleeping in his shack where she'd be bound to look for him, he'd just wrap up and lie on the beach.

Mrs. Thomson gave a furious and outraged snort but she made no comment.

He had gone to get a blanket, saw someone had been messing with his things, and he began to hunt around. He had fallen over this guy who was sprawled out at the foot of a coconut palm, knocked out. He poured some water on him and he came to and asked for help. Seemed dazed like.

Sergeant Clay waited patiently until Paxton had finished the coffee, holding the hot cup in both shaking hands to steady it.

"Feel better? I'd like to ask you some questions."

Paxton smiled. "I'll do my best but I don't guarantee anything." Except for a tiny slit, one eye was closed, his cheek was badly bruised and skinned.

"Now, then, what happened to you, Mr. Paxton?"

"I don't know."

"You don't know who hit you?"

"Is that what happened? How did I get there—under a tree?" His good eye traveled slowly around the room, rested on me. "You've been hurt, too." He studied me anxiously. "Not badly, I hope. Who was it, the prowler?"

I was too bewildered to answer.

"Let's get it straight," the sergeant said. "When did you rent a trailer here? According to Miss Quarles, you have that one next door."

Paxton hesitated. Then he grinned sheepishly. "Well, I guess I might as well tell you the truth. I'm flat broke. My health failed some months ago, one lung collapsed, and I had to give up my job. I headed south and began to run out of what savings I had. So, finally, these past two weeks, I've been sleeping on the beach to stretch what money I had left so I could use it for food. Then, yesterday, I ran out entirely—and if you can find a thin dime on me, it's more than I can do —and when I hit this place and found there was no one around I kept an eye on it. The idea of sleeping in a real bed was more of a temptation than I could withstand." He smiled again, embarrassed but half-amused, too. "And then Miss Quarles graciously offered to share her dinner with me and practically saved my life."

"And then what happened?"

For the first time Paxton was at a loss. He looked at me and raised his eyebrows.

"It's all right," I assured him. "I told them about

finding the necklace in the icebox." Certainly that was the reasonable thing to say, but it sounded for all the world as though I was prompting him.

"Yes. Well, that was quite a find. They were beautiful stones. But you'll know that better than I do, probably. I'm no expert."

"As no one else has seen the necklace," the sergeant commented dryly, "we have no opinion."

Paxton gave me a startled look. "What happened to it?"

"We are discussing your movements now," Clay reminded him, and again Paxton looked startled.

"Mine? Oh, of course. Well, there's not much more to say. That little dog the boy had picked up began to bark like mad and it woke the kid. Miss Quarles had promised to look after him, so she ran over there. I waited for her to return and then I realized she had taken the boy back to his parents' trailer—he'd gone out looking for the dog—and that she had decided to stay with him. So, of course, I left."

"And then what?"

"That's all. I don't even remember being struck. I left Miss Quarles's trailer. I woke up when the Indian threw water over me. Period."

"I see you've scorched your trousers. How did that happen?"

Paxton stretched out his legs, looked down in surprise. "I have no idea. They were all right last time I noticed them."

"Brother, you must have been out," commented the trooper at the door.

"Did you ever hear of a man named Kenyon? Jack Kenyon?"

Paxton blinked at Clay, shook his head, and then clutched it with both hands. "Next time," he predicted, "it's going to fall off."

"Brown?"

"Brown what?"

"Ever know a man named Brown?"

This time Paxton checked the head shake. "Probably. Everyone knows someone named Brown. Classmate in college. A fellow who lives in the same apartment building."

"Can you describe them?"

"College man is tall and thin and red-haired. The other one is—I don't know—just ordinary. About my size. Wears thick glasses."

"Let's take a little walk," Clay suggested. "There are a couple of people I want you to see."

Paxton got up cautiously. For a moment he stood swaying, looking down at me. "I hope you are all right. You look to me as though you ought to see a doctor." With the sergeant's hand to steady him, he went out. After a moment's hesitation Grant followed them.

"So you was telling the truth," Mrs. Thomson said in a tone of profound surprise. "That guy was here all the time, like you said, and using my trailer without intending to pay a cent. I could sue him for that."

"Of course she was telling the truth," Charles said. "Mary." When I made no reply he shook me lightly. "Mary!"

"Charles, if Paxton is telling the truth, there's no one left, is there? The sergeant is going to take me to town. He's going to hold me as a material witness."

"When we get to town," Charles said, "I'll find out just how soon we can get married in Florida. You are a born victim. I want the legal right to look out for you before something else happens."

"What do you think is going to happen?" Clay asked smoothly from the doorway. "And you aren't going to get married until this case is solved—if then. Husbands and wives can't be forced to testify against each other, MacIntosh. I suppose a legal man like you overlooked that little point."

13

A siren snarled, a blinker flashed on top of a car, a motor raced, stopped, and car doors slammed. There was a rumble of men's voices and then, unexpectedly, a laugh, high and sweet. There was no mistaking Sonia's voice.

"All so mysterious," she was saying. "I think troopers are divine but I hope you are going to tell me what this is all about. I'm simply wild with curiosity."

I was so angry that I forgot everything except the point that stuck out a mile. "You didn't tell her!" I raged to Sergeant Clay. "You've let her come out here without warning her or preparing her for Jack's murder. Of all the cruel, heartless things to do!"

Imperturbable as he had appeared up to now, except for that one irritable explosion over the noise from the Browns' television set, he was taken aback by my outburst. For a moment, speaking to Charles, he had had the air of a man who had the situation under control. He started to speak, looked at me rather queerly; then he shrugged and turned to go out.

"Wait," I implored him, "don't let her see Jack until you've broken it to her. She's so in love with him. It isn't fair to—"

"Quiet." He wasn't even paying attention to me. He was listening to the voices outside.

Sonia was speaking again, the laughter gone, her voice sad. "I guess I really know what it's all about. Poor darling Mary! We've tried so hard to guard her, to look after her, but people like that, if you don't watch every minute— I've been so terribly worried." There was a break in the warm, sweet voice. "Especially that public scandal in Lloydsville about her drinking. That's when I began to realize how bad it was."

The sergeant shook off my restraining hand, went outside. "You are Miss Sonia Colette, aren't you? I am Sergeant Clay."

"That's just my professional name. I am Sarah Kenyon, Mrs. John Kenyon. Your men were so mysterious, Sergeant. They just asked me to come out here. They wouldn't say why. But I'm glad it's someone like you, someone who will know how to handle her. Someone strong and understanding." There was a little catch in her breath. "Tell me—what has she done?"

"You figured she had been doing something, Mrs. Kenyon?" Sergeant Clay asked, and I saw Charles smile grimly.

"Well, only if she had been drinking, of course. Otherwise she wouldn't hurt a fly."

I pulled away from Charles who had caught hold of my hand, and listened to that sweet, poisonous voice, knowing exactly what was happening. No man could resist her. The sergeant already believed I was a liar if not a murderer. For a bitter moment there seemed to be no solid ground left, nothing I could trust.

"In here, please."

Sergeant Clay moved to one side and Sonia came into the trailer. She wore a thin white dress that made her look about fifteen. Her hair was pulled back in a simple roll, the way I usually wore mine. She had almost no makeup. She looked like the girl on old-fashioned candy boxes, like the one in illustrations who stands under a shower of apple blossoms, like a daffodil.

She stood, half-smiling, and turned from Mrs. Mer-

cer to Mrs. Thomson, from the Seminole to Charles.
And then she saw me.

"Mary!" She stood stock still, her face drained of
color. Then she took an uncertain step toward me,
those lovely eyes of hers searching my face. "Mary,
what happened to you?"

I tried to speak but no sound would come out. It
seemed to me that I had never really seen her before,
never before known that she was dangerous.

She was also a better actress than I had ever realized. She had expected to find me dead, to find me
beside the dead body of Jack's partner. And, instead,
I was very much alive. She must have been screaming
aloud inside that still, lovely face, wondering what had
happened.

"Now, Mrs. Kenyon," Sergeant Clay said, "you
identify her as your cousin, Mary Quarles?"

"Why, of course."

"I understand you and your husband have been
taking care of her."

"We tried," she said softly.

"Suppose you tell me how she happened to come
out here. Sit down, Mrs. Kenyon."

The trooper at the door and the Seminole lounging
against the wall were watching her the way men always watched her. Mrs. Mercer studied her as though
she were a coiled rattler. Mrs. Thomson looked from
me to Sonia and back again with a puzzled expression.
Only Charles's eyes remained cold and alert.

There was a small frown between Sonia's brows
and she automatically smoothed it away. She put one
small hand appealingly on the sergeant's sleeve. "Must
we—can't we talk somewhere else?"

She hadn't been prepared to force the issue in my
presence. Between us lay all the twenty-four years of
my life, all the shared memories. Whatever had happened to her, she did not want to destroy that, not
with my eyes on her, not when we were face to face.
Perhaps the plan she and Jack had created between

them had seemed no more than a theatrical illusion,
a harmless piece of stagecraft, when I was at a distance.

"We'll be going back to town in a few minutes," the
sergeant told her. "We have just a few things to clear
up here first." His face wore the dazed look men had
when they saw Sonia. "You don't mind?"

He pulled out a wicker chair with a gallantry that
had been conspicuously lacking in his treatment of
me, though he had been polite enough. Sonia sat
down with that easy grace she had acquired with her
stage training. A rough edge of the chair snagged her
skirt, pulling it halfway up her thigh. She sat watching
the sergeant like an obedient child and did not appear
to notice it. She wore no slip under her dress.

"Oh, no. I only want to help. But if you could tell
me what is wrong—"

"We'll come to that." The sergeant was looking
with undisguised interest at the display of sun-tanned
leg. She wore no stockings, either, but not many
women do in Florida.

"Now then." The sergeant produced his notebook
and removed his eyes from Sonia's legs. "I believe Miss
Quarles came out here today, at your suggestion, to
spend the night in your husband's Scotty. Correct?"

Sonia turned big startled eyes on Clay. "Why, no.
She has been out here for several days."

"Yeah," Mrs. Thomson broke in. "That's what I've
been telling you. Three days."

Clay put up his hand in the familiar gesture. "Later,
Mrs. Thomson. Well, Mrs. Kenyon?"

"You see"—Sonia's hands twisted together—"there
had been a little trouble. That is, Mary got involved
—that is, she had been drinking rather heavily and she
was involved in some sort of scandal in Lloydsville.
That's the little town in New York where we both
grew up."

She gave Clay her famous smile. "A dear little town
but rather straitlaced. Anyhow, we realized—that is,

Jack and I talked it over—there wasn't anyone else to help her, you know. So we thought if she came to us, we might be able to give her a new start in life. That's all she needs. Truly it is, Sergeant."

She was keeping her eyes fixed on Clay's face. Not once had she looked at me. Only the twitching at the corners of her mouth, the tightness with which she was clenching her hands in her lap, revealed that she was facing a situation for which she had not been prepared. If Charles's deductions were right, my presence, cold sober, must be having a shattering effect on her.

"So Jack brought her out here to that darling little trailer. He—we thought, you know, that with the ocean for bathing and the beach for sun and no—bad company or anything like that, we could get her so she would be all right. Lots of people are cured, you know."

"Mary," MacIntosh broke in before Clay could silence him—or perhaps Clay hadn't tried very hard to silence him, "let's clear up the problem of where you spent those last two nights before you came here and met your cousin. The motels would have your name, wouldn't they, and your car-license number?"

The tension around Sonia's mouth relaxed. For the first time she met my eyes. She was smiling faintly. And then I remembered. The Kenyons had known all along, of course, because of my daily telephone calls during the trip. But it was the one thing I had forgotten to tell Charles. Such a childish thing, really. Such an utterly and completely fatal thing.

"I didn't stay at motels the last few nights." Because of the cold, my voice had an ugly croak. "After the ice and the storms up north, it was so wonderful to be out in the air that I wrapped up in a coat and slept on the beach under the stars."

"God!" After a moment Charles asked, and there was fear in his voice, "Where was this?"

"The first time I wasn't far from St. Augustine. The second night I stayed near Daytona Beach."

"And no one saw you?"

I shook my head. "If there had been anyone around, I wouldn't have risked it. I'm sorry, Charles. There's no possible way I can prove that I wasn't here. I know just how idiotic it was, just how disastrous. But that is what I did."

"But the Kenyons knew?"

"Oh, yes. When I said I was going to try it, they thought it was very funny and encouraged me to go ahead."

"That's not true," Sonia exclaimed. "We would never have encouraged such a thing. And, anyhow, she was here."

Clay jotted down a note, got to his feet. My heart thumped. He was going to arrest me now. Instead, he turned to Sonia. "Mrs. Kenyon, would you mind coming with me?"

"Why not at all, Sergeant." She reached down automatically to release her snagged skirt, and preceded him out of the trailer.

I clutched at Charles's hand. "He's going to show her Jack's body. He should have warned her."

"Do you still care what happens to that woman?"

"You don't understand. She's in love with him. This is needlessly cruel and I don't like cruelty."

"You are a pushover, aren't you? Little Sonia is selling you down the river as hard and fast as she can; she deserves everything that is coming to her. But why in hell didn't you tell me you had slept for two nights on the beach?"

"I didn't think of it," I said inadequately.

"You didn't—am I going to marry an imbecile?"

"I guess I just sort of lost my head."

"You can say that again. Of all the cockeyed things to do! Aside from the fact that you might have been molested—or God knows what."

"Well, I wasn't."

The flashlights and the voices were back of the Browns' trailer, near the car with its horrible occupant.

I heard Sonia's high, sweet voice. "No, I'm quite sure, Sergeant. I never saw the man before. I have never heard Jack speak of anyone named Brown. I'm positive he doesn't know him. But we can ask him when we get back to the hotel."

"That's right. I meant to ask you where your husband is."

"The poor lamb is doubled up in bed with some kind of food poisoning. He couldn't even go on tonight. I had to change our routine and do imitations." Her voice rose. "But what happened to this man Brown? Who killed him? Not—surely not Mary?"

Clay made no reply. "The Scotty belongs to your husband, doesn't it? Do you mind—are you all right, Mrs. Kenyon?"

"It's just a kind of belated shock. Seeing that awful sight. Yes, I'll be all right, Sergeant."

They were going toward the Scotty now. Then I heard Sonia's scream, wild and terrible. "Jack! Jack! O God, it's Jack!"

I covered my ears with my hands, trying to shut out that frantic voice. Whatever she was, Sonia had loved Jack. Her grief seemed to be tearing at my own flesh. Beside me I felt Charles stiffen and I looked up as Paxton came in with Grant. The latter eased him into a chair.

For a moment Paxton closed his eyes. Then he opened them and took a long breath. He looked at me groggily. "I feel punch-drunk. Two murders. On top of that, I've been knocked out and you—what did happen to you, Miss Quarles? And that woman screaming—what else has been going on?"

"My cousin Sonia has just seen her husband's body. They didn't even warn her."

"That's tough. Nasty sight for anyone. I didn't know them but I was pretty shook up myself when I got a look at those two bodies."

There were stumbling footsteps outside, then Sergeant Clay helped Sonia into the trailer. For a moment she stood clinging to his arm and then she pitched over in a dead faint.

"Don't lift her head," I said. "Put some pillows under her feet. Charles, get a—"

"Here," Mrs. Mercer said. "I have this little bottle of smelling salts." She pulled a tiny jeweled bottle out of her handbag and I held it to Sonia's nose, taking her wrist, aware of her ice-cold hand, of the thin and thready pulse. Her hand had been like that, I remembered, when I had left her at the hotel. The terror in her eyes was understandable now. She had been looking ahead to murder.

"No, Charles, not a drink. She's in shock. Get a blanket. We've got to warm her up, somehow."

The sergeant helped me wrap the blanket around her. There were dark shadows under her eyes. Then I felt her cold hand twitch, saw her lids flutter, her lips move.

"What caused all this hell?" Paxton demanded suddenly. "Was all this because of the diamond necklace? What a senseless tragedy! Worth enough to keep two people in clover and, instead, two people are dead."

"It makes you think," Mrs. Thomson said.

"What I'm thinking," Mrs. Mercer said grimly, "is that I'd like to know what happened to the money Glenn was supposed to be carrying. He must have been loaded."

"It's bound to get back in the right hands," Paxton said. "I think you can trust the police for that. It will go where it belongs."

"But whose hands?" Mrs. Mercer asked. "I have some rights here."

Sonia's eyes opened, looked straight at me. "Mary," she said brokenly "why did you? Jack tried so hard to help you. Why?"

14

For a long moment Sonia and I stared at each other, the past dead between us, but knowing each other better than we ever had before and aware of that bitter knowledge.

Little by little, the color had seeped back into her lips, but the hand I still held unconsciously was icy to the touch. I dropped her wrist but as she started to lift her head, I said sharply, "Don't move yet. You're in shock."

"Do you wonder? Seeing Jack like that. Do you wonder?"

Behind those wonderful blue eyes there was horror and a kind of stunned disbelief. This could not have happened to her. Things had always worked out as she had planned. But her mind had begun to function again; I had seen that in the appraising look she gave me. What she still had not faced was her own involvement in the plan that had led to Jack's death. I wondered whether she ever would. Sonia's capacity for self-deception, as I was beginning to grasp, was bottomless.

"Mrs. Kenyon," Sergeant Clay began, his voice gentle but determined, "I'll have to ask you some questions as soon as you are ready."

"It's not fair to question her yet," I protested.

"What are you afraid of, Mary?"

The gauntlet had been flung down now. Whatever personal shock and grief and loss she felt, whatever the upheaval caused by the wreckage of those carefully wrought plans that had gone so frightfully askew, she had made her decision, decided to play out the game with such trumps as she still held.

But what cards did she have? Jack was dead. The necklace had disappeared. All she could salvage now would be the fragments of her reputation. And that meant, basically, opposing my story to hers. Not such a bad hand, after all. Anyone looking from her, sweet and wan, lovely and helpless, to me, with my battered face and swollen nose and croaking voice, would give her the game.

At last she looked away from me, turned to the sergeant. "Why did she do it? She's not drunk."

"Is it true," Clay asked unexpectedly, "that your husband took all your cousin's money and sent her out here penniless?"

I was as surprised by the question as Sonia was. "Jack didn't take it, Sergeant; he borrowed it for a few days. Didn't Mary explain that? He just borrowed it. He'll"—a spasm caught her throat—"he would have returned it on Monday. After all, she didn't need anything here and we were awfully hard up. Mary, you know, got everything when Aunt Jane died. Everything. Of course, she was with her all the time; she was bound to influence a helpless old woman like that."

Helpless? Aunt Jane? I was about to protest when Charles touched my arm warningly with his hand. He hadn't even looked at me but he knew that I was going to speak, and for some reason he didn't want me to. He was watching Sonia now, his face granite-hard.

"Suppose you start from the beginning and tell me why you thought it best for Miss Quarles to come here."

Sonia's brows puckered in thought. She moved her head restlessly, staring up at Clay. "Can't I sit up or at least have a pillow under my head?" she asked fretfully.

Clay lifted her head and shoulders, put pillows under them. Half-lying, half-sitting on the floor, she looked helpless and fragile.

"Well," she began, "Mary and I were brought up by Aunt Jane after our parents died. We were both orphans. Then—I didn't like depending so much on dear Aunt Jane who had taken care of us since we were little girls. I thought it was time to be responsible for myself, to relieve her of some of the burden. So I left Lloydsville to be on my own. Where I got the courage I can't imagine now. I was only seventeen. Mary stayed with Aunt Jane. In a way, I can understand that. She was supported without having to work and Aunt Jane was a very wealthy woman."

As Sonia went on, I had a half-embarrassed feeling that she had watched too many soap operas. She had, as she told her story, married unhappily ("I was just a baby, really"), struggled to the top of the ladder through a number of vicissitudes, and then she and Jack had discovered each other, married in spite of the fact that it meant professional ruin for him, and had been divinely happy.

Mary hadn't married. For some reason she had never been very attractive to men. She had grown restless, waiting for Aunt Jane to die, and she had begun to drink heavily. Rumors about her behavior had reached Sonia but she had refused to credit them. People, she told Clay earnestly, could be so uncharitable. But then the scandal had been made public and she had urged Mary to come down where she and Jack could watch out for her and try to get her back on an even keel.

I kept reminding myself that I was the woman Sonia was describing, but it didn't seem real to me.

So, she went on, Mary had come to Florida, and Jack had brought her out here to the trailer park three days ago, and he had been going back and forth, making sure that she was all right, that she wasn't getting herself into trouble.

"Just like I told you," Mrs. Thomson put in. "Just

like I said. Making scenes, acting mean, drunk as a coot one day."

"I understand Mr. Kenyon left a bottle of bourbon for Miss Quarles. Isn't that rather extraordinary in the circumstances?"

"Well, we understood people shouldn't be forced to stop completely, that they should just taper off or they might have some sort of nervous breakdown. We meant to do the right thing."

"You lent her some of your clothes, didn't you?"

"Mine?" Sonia said in surprise. "Why, no. Mary had her own clothes, of course." For a moment her eyes rested, puzzled, on Charles's cumbersome sweater and slacks which I was wearing.

Clay scrawled something on a piece of paper and gave it to Grant who went out. When the door opened I could hear sounds of activity. Cars were starting up. Men were talking. Incongruously, someone laughed, a great belly laugh, as though he had just heard the end of a good story.

I realized that the two bodies, after having been photographed and fingerprinted and whatever else had to be done, were being moved to an ambulance to be taken back to town.

That knowledge was in Sonia's face, too. She turned her head on her arm and broke into long, shuddering sobs. "Not Jack!" Her voice rose to a high, thin wail. "Not Jack!"

When the sounds of the motors had died away, she sat up, dried her tears, sipped a glass of water handed her by Clay and then, with his help, got onto a chair, her small hands gripped the arms. For once, with her hair disheveled, her face stained with tears, lids reddened, without makeup, the beauty seemed to have drained from her. She was haggard. This, I realized with a sense of shock, was how she would look when she was old.

"Do you know this man, Mrs. Kenyon?"

She followed Clay's gesture to Paxton, who was

leaning forward in his chair listening to the conversation with the puzzled air of a man who has come in at the last act of a play and is trying to piece the plot together. She shook her head.

"You've never seen him before?"

Again she shook her head. Then that dazzling smile lighted her face. "I'd remember."

"What do you know about a diamond necklace that was found in your husband's trailer?"

"A diamond necklace! That's ridiculous. We couldn't afford a diamond necklace. Why even my engagement ring"—and she held out her hand, showing a ring with a modest solitaire—"was all that Jack could afford. I think it's sweet; I wouldn't want anything more. He couldn't buy a diamond necklace!"

"According to Miss Quarles, she found one in the icebox drain in your husband's trailer."

"Yes, I can testify to that," Paxton put in. "I saw the thing myself. Beautiful stones they seemed to be."

"What did you do with it, Mr. Paxton?"

His eyebrows arched in astonishment. "Nothing. When Miss Quarles went over to look after the little boy, I decided not to wait any longer in her trailer. Last time I saw the necklace it was on the drainboard beside the sink."

"There really was a necklace?" Sonia looked bewildered.

"I found it," I told her, "and Brown told me he had come here to buy it from Jack and he said you knew all about the deal."

"Oh, Mary." There was only weary rejection in her voice.

"I can say this," Mrs. Mercer put in, "Glenn thought Miss Quarles was Sonia Colette. We both did."

"I've done a lot of listening," Clay said unexpectedly.

"You've listened to Mrs. Kenyon," Charles told him. "A highly moving account of her Youthful Struggles, her Giving Up All for Love, and how the Wicked and Debauched Cousin defrauded her of Her Inheritance." The parody in his voice stung Sonia but she was under tight control now. The big blue eyes watched him reproachfully.

"Will Sonia reach the peak of her ambitions? *Will* Mary succeed in undermining her with dear Aunt Jane? See our next thrilling installment of this real-life drama."

Instead of interrupting, Clay leaned back in his chair as though he had all the time in the world. He was giving Charles a lot of rope, I thought uneasily.

"Look here," Paxton protested, "this is none of my business, Sergeant, but this guy is way out of line. Mrs. Kenyon has had a terrible shock. I don't think he should be allowed to treat her with so little common decency, so little respect for her grief and loss."

I had noticed, without too much disillusionment, that Paxton's attitude toward me had changed as a result of my altered appearance. After his initial concern, he had viewed Charles's clothes and my battered face with a kind of distaste. It was Sonia who was arousing all his chivalry now.

Her famous smile illuminated her tired face. "Thank you," she said gently.

"I'd like to get across my version of this story." Charles spoke directly to Clay, ignoring Paxton's protest, ignoring Sonia.

"I'm listening," Clay said. He added, "But I have a kind of weakness for evidence. So far—"

"There's been a shortage of proof. Well, we'll get you some, Sergeant. But first I'd like to start with that soap opera, the Trials and Tribulations of Sonia Colette. I've been checking up on her for weeks. She left Lloydsville at seventeen, with a married man in his fifties. This, not unnaturally, prejudiced the man's wife against her. Her second wedding broke up another long-standing marriage. For the unsavory scandal that has always accompanied Sonia Colette's name, I refer you to the newspapers, of which I have made an exhaustive study. You'll find them interesting.

"Now, when we come to her third marriage, to Jack Kenyon, the situation is somewhat different. Kenyon's contract called for him to remain unmarried because he was a drawing card with women, so every effort was made to keep that marriage a dead secret. But someone revealed it to a Hollywood gossip columnist."

"This is all very entertaining," Clay said, "but we have a couple of murders to solve here."

"I'm trying to help you solve them. Those two deaths didn't result from spontaneous combustion at the trailer park tonight. They grew out of a situation that has been building up for some time. I'm not wasting your time; I'm trying to help you save time."

"Go ahead and save some."

"Kenyon's specialty was boyish charm, but as he grew older—he was forty-four when he was killed— it had lost its impact on girls and he had to rely more and more on older women to provide the kind of popularity he needed. Kenyon was willing to do a lot to maintain that popularity. Quite a lot. And he found women of—shall I say more mature charms?— grateful. And generous. So generous, on the whole, that his career as a night-club singer wasn't of any particular interest to him except in so far as it brought him to the attention of the ladies, his real source of income."

Watching Clay steadily, Charles told him the story he had told me of Jack's partnership with a man who screened prospects for him, making sure that they were wealthy and too vulnerable to be able to afford publicity or exposure. That had been the situation with his client, whose interests he was representing here. She had gone to Las Vegas, had fallen in a big way for Jack Kenyon, and had had a passing but hectic affair with him.

Sonia stiffened. "That's a lie!"

"It was her diamond necklace that he stole when the affair was over. She didn't want to take any steps because she was still in love with him, but when she heard about his marriage to Sonia, she hit the roof. She had me trace Kenyon and sent me here to get back that necklace. Now here we enter the field of speculation."

"We've never left it," Clay told him.

"We'll find some nice concrete evidence to support this structure of conjecture," Charles assured him. "But I can at least tell you what I think happened. When Sonia married Jack Kenyon she didn't like the idea of their splitting the money from the jewel thefts. So Kenyon double-crossed his partner and held on to the necklace. In retaliation, the partner disclosed their marriage. Who else could have done it? He's the only person who was close enough to either of them to know of it."

"When you get out on a limb, brother," Clay commented half admiringly, "you get way out. Now this mythical partner—"

"Or, if you prefer names, why not say Paxton?"

15

Paxton leaped about a foot off his chair and then sank back, clutching his head.

"This is ridiculous," Sonia cried. "I've never even seen him before. It's horrible, the things that man is saying about Jack. About me. Stop him, Sergeant. Stop him. Jack and I adored each other. There were no other women. And if you think he'd do a thing like that for money—that he'd rob women—" -

"Don't let the guy stampede you, Mrs. Kenyon." Paxton was angry.

"If you've finished—" Clay said.

"I haven't finished with that soap opera." Charles said. "And here is where Mary Quarles was brought into this unsavory mess. Not long ago her aunt died, leaving her some property and all her money. Mary made a will, with her cousin as her sole heir. Then she wrote Sonia to say that she was going to marry a man named Richard Burgess. That meant that a nice piece of change and some property would undoubtedly go to her future husband. So the Kenyons went into action."

He recapitulated my story of the evening at the country club when Gus had doped my drink and how the story had leaked out to the Town Crier.

He turned on Sonia. "How did you happen to know about that little episode, Mrs. Kenyon? No one had time to write you. You telephoned her immediately after the Town Crier had made her position in Lloydsville unpleasant. How did you know?"

She gaped at him.

Charles did not wait for an answer. He kept hammering away at Clay. "You probably won't get much out of the broadcaster. Those boys protect their sources. But—what's the name of the bartender at the country club, Mary?"

"Gus. Gus Futrell."

"Find him, Sergeant. Find out who paid him for that job. Another thing, check the flask in Kenyon's pocket. If it isn't loaded with some drug, I'll eat my hat. If he hadn't been killed before he could move in on Mary, she would be dead in that Scotty right now and her fingerprints would be on the weapon that was supposed to have killed Paxton."

Paxton rubbed his forehead in perplexity. "Will you tell me what I'm supposed to have to do with all this? Why on earth anyone would want to kill me?"

"The Kenyons knew you could blow them sky-high with what you knew about their activities. They wanted you out of the way. Permanently. I think they lured you here with that necklace. What they intended, of course, was to get Mary here and have her take the rap when Kenyon killed you."

"Well, it's a good story," Clay said.

"Sergeant," Sonia cried, "you don't believe him! You can't possibly believe him."

"You've got some pieces left over in this puzzle of yours, haven't you, MacIntosh?"

"What pieces?"

"Well, there's the man Brown. Where does he fit in?"

"Brown," Charles said promptly, "was the fence to whom Kenyon expected to sell the necklace. Brown told Mary so himself. But unfortunately, just as this double cross was set up and timed to go off, Brown sent word that he was on his way to meet Kenyon at the trailer park. Kenyon must have been having fits. One thing had to be avoided at all costs. Paxton and

Brown must not meet. And, besides, Mary was sober when she was on the beach; she had to have time to become drunk before Paxton could be killed.

"So, while Paxton was hiding out in that empty trailer, waiting for a chance to get the necklace—he must be the one who searched the Scotty while you were on the beach, Mary—Kenyon was on the prowl. He put the telephone and the cars out of commission, except for Brown's, and then sat back to wait for Paxton to take the bait.

"Well, Paxton finally went to the Scotty but he must have been alerted to the possibility of a double cross. He knew the Kenyons. Mary left him conveniently alone in the Scotty, after having found the necklace, so when Kenyon came in, Paxton was waiting with the steak knife."

Sonia caught in her breath with a sharp hiss. She was paper white. I didn't blame her. Something in Charles's words had conjured up an ugly picture, making it much too graphic. Paxton looked angry and baffled. Clay simply listened.

"Sergeant," Paxton said with a helpless gesture, "this is the damnedest nonsense I've ever heard. Doesn't it strike you as unlikely, to say the least, that I'd hang around here after committing a murder?"

Charles grinned. "I'll bet twenty to one Kenyon put your car out of commission along with the others— and you couldn't go far on foot, not in this country. Anyhow, you had a reason for hanging around. You remembered that, while no one else in the trailer park had seen you, Mary could identify you. That is what you intended to remedy. You hid in the empty trailer and watched for her to come back. Only I was right on her heels. Then I went into the trailer and you knocked me out. That gave you a clear field and you got one of those pleasant surprises. You saw that illuminating interview between Brown and Mary, discovered he was Kenyon's fence, and prepared to buy the necklace. You waited until Mary got away from him, then you closed in. So you had both the necklace and the money."

"And then," Paxton said gently, "I knocked myself out."

"Of course you did," Charles retorted. "You had accidentally started a fire by dropping a match in that gasoline. You couldn't get away, so you had to bluff it out. But I have a hunch that you overdid it when you slammed yourself against that tree trunk. Hard to estimate the force of anything like that, isn't it? You may regret hitting yourself quite so hard. Feeling a bit sick and dizzy, aren't you? Finding it hard to focus."

Surely, I thought, Clay is going to point out the weakness in Charles's story, the one overwhelming fact that makes it all nonsense. I had been waiting, sick at heart, for Clay to stop him, handcuff him, take him away, but Clay was still noncommittal, letting us all talk, giving nothing away. So I had to point out the thing they seemed not to realize, and I wished I was dead.

"Sergeant," I croaked, stopped to blow my nose. I was shaking with cold but I was hot, too. "Sergeant, it can't be true—not the way Charles is telling it. Oh, about the necklace, perhaps, and Jack and Sonia wanting to discredit me. But not about the murders."

"Keep still, Mary," Charles shouted. "As your lawyer—"

"You aren't my lawyer, Charles. You aren't—anything at all but a stranger I met here. A stranger who wanted a necklace. Sonia—whatever she is, whatever she has done—loved Jack. This story is impossible." I turned to Clay. "Can't you see that for yourself? She wouldn't sit here and provide cover for a man who, she believed, had murdered her own husband. Never in the world."

I braced myself to look at Charles. He was smiling broadly. "You are a nice girl, Mary. A born victim but a nice girl. You forget just how much little Sonia has at stake: a diamond necklace; an unknown amount of cash; a career—however shaky it may be at the moment; a reputation—however tarnished; and a natural desire to escape being an accessory in a first-degree murder charge. Use your head, girl, and your eyes and your ears. That's what they are for. She walked in here, took one look at Paxton, knew the score, and fainted."

"I had just seen my husband's dead body," Sonia said somberly. "Everyone seems to forget that."

"And as soon as she began to come out of it, Paxton made his bid. You all heard him. How did he put it: something about two people being able to live in clover on that necklace. An assurance the money would get into the right hands. In other words, a promise that if she kept her mouth shut, he would split the proceeds with her."

"I don't believe it," I said stubbornly.

"Look, you little idiot, don't you realize you are doing your best to put a noose around your own neck?" He turned to Clay. "Can you think of one single reason why Mary would have killed Jack Kenyon? I can testify that, until I turned his head, she had assumed that the dead man was Paxton. Do you imagine for a minute she could stab a man in a fifteen-foot trailer without knowing his identity?"

Clay made no comment. I didn't understand him. He didn't look or act like an incompetent man but he was letting us all talk too much. Did he expect that, in the long run, one of us would convict himself? What kind of game was he playing?

"Another thing," Charles went on, "do you believe the smartest state's attorney in the country could convince twelve good men and true that this girl beat Brown to death the way he was beaten? What was her motive? How could she handle a man twice her weight, even assuming that she is either a judo artist or an Amazon?"

"There's plenty of motive," Clay said lazily. "The beating Brown gave her, the diamond necklace, the money Brown was carrying. And, of course, she didn't need to be an Amazon. Not with your help."

"So we were in it together," Charles said. "If either of us took the necklace and the money, where are they now?"

"We'll find them," Clay said confidently.

"I suppose Mary also put the cars and the telephone out of commission?"

"Are you hiding behind a woman, MacIntosh?" That wasn't really very clever if Clay expected to get a rise out of Charles who merely grinned at him. The sergeant got up. "If you have no more suggestions, we'll be getting back to town now."

"Are you arresting Mary and me?"

"That seems to be the general idea."

"Mary isn't going to jail," Charles said tightly. "Even when she is cleared, as she will be, that kind of thing sticks." He reached in his pocket and pulled out a notebook and pen. He wrote swiftly, tore the sheet out and handed it to the sergeant. "That's my client. There's a limit to everything. Please call her at once. She'll have to verify my story and tell you exactly why I came here."

The sergeant consulted his watch. "Four o'clock. That means one in California. She'll be asleep."

"Then wake her up."

Clay handed the paper to Grant who went out again. For a long time the living room of the trailer was quiet. Clay seemed content to wait indefinitely. He was a very patient man, or a very wily one.

The first sound was a huge and noisy yawn from Mrs. Thomson. The Seminole stood almost without moving but he had missed nothing. He was getting a glimpse of white civilization and I wondered what he thought of it. Mrs. Mercer, on the other hand, had not once stopped moving. She changed position constantly, crossed and uncrossed her legs, her fingers beat a tattoo on the chair arm, she fidgeted with her hair, with a charm bracelet, with her rings. She picked up and put down her big handbag. She even made a careful repair of her makeup. Sonia was leaning back in her chair, eyes nearly closed, but I felt sure she was watching us all closely.

Clay stirred. "How do you account for your husband coming out here, Mrs. Kenyon, since he was suffering from food poisoning? Doesn't it seem strange to you, if he was well enough to drive to the park, that he didn't go on with his act, that he didn't at least inform you of his change of plans?"

"I simply can't understand it. Unless Mary called him. I just don't know."

"The telephone here was out of order," Charles said. "Mary couldn't have called him."

"Would you care to change your story about your cousin coming here three days ago?"

Sonia shook her head.

"And your story about your husband's movements?"

"But I can't change my story. I don't understand why Jack came here tonight. He was just miserable when I left him to go to work."

"When was the last time you saw him?"

"Why—I'm not sure—I—" She put her hands over her eyes, began to cry. "I've had such a shock, Sergeant. I can't stand any more right now."

"We can wait," he said in his relaxed tone.

She sat bolt upright, looking startled. "Sergeant, I've just remembered. Jack and I have a booking in Arizona for three weeks. We are to leave Monday. We—even without Jack I'll have to go. We had so little money that I can't afford not to take that job. I'll have to go on working, supporting myself."

If it had been ditchdigging, she couldn't have made it sound more difficult.

Clay gave her a speculative look. "There have been two murders here, Mrs. Kenyon. We've got to have all the answers before we can permit you to leave. Anyhow, you will naturally want to make arrangements for your husband's funeral, as soon as the body is released."

"You mean I can't go?" Anger flamed in her face and then she forced it back. "Please, Sergeant," she begged him, "you don't understand how important it is. When the papers get this story, it's going to do me a lot of harm professionally unless I am right under a spotlight so people can see for themselves that I am in the clear."

"It would take a lot of courage, wouldn't it, to put on a gay act so few days after your husband's murder?"

"Stage people always pride themselves on the fact that 'the show must go on.' I could tell you the most wonderful stories; for instance, an actress did a wildly funny show just an hour after she learned her son had been killed in battle and—"

"Sorry, Mrs. Kenyon, I can't make the decision to let you go. I have no authority to do it."

Grant came in with a rolled-up newspaper which he put down on Clay's lap, looked at him and went out.

Clay opened it slowly and I saw the hammer, with blood and hairs on the end. He put it down where we could all see it. Then he looked more closely at the handle.

"Anyone recognize this?"

No one spoke.

"Now that's odd, you know," Clay said in a conversational tone. "That M burned into the handle. Just like all the other tools in your toolbox, isn't it, MacIntosh?"

Charles's face was stiff. "I don't know. I haven't examined it."

Grant was back again, a piece of paper in his hand. "This call was just completed, Sergeant."

Clay seemed to take an interminable time reading

the few lines of writing. "Well, MacIntosh, your so-called client, Mrs. Klenneman, says that you do not represent her; in fact, she never heard of you. At least, it was a nice try."

16

Grant had taken up his former position at the door. I was aware of the growing tension, aware that the trooper no longer lounged, he was ready for action. It seemed to me that the air in the house trailer was becoming heavy, curiously hard to breathe.

Clay stood up, looked from Mrs. Thomson to the Seminole. "You two can go now, but don't leave the county without permission."

The Seminole went out promptly, without a backward glance. Mrs. Thomson was reluctant to miss anything. She hovered until a sharp word from Clay made the trooper stand back and gesture toward the door.

"I don't know a thing about this," Mrs. Mercer said as the sergeant turned to her.

"I don't think she does either," I put in, ignoring Charles's imploring, "Mary, for God's sake, keep your mouth shut."

"We'll have to get your testimony in writing. Will you pack a bag? We'll put you up at the hotel for the night." Clay looked at me. "There's plenty of room at the hotel."

"My packing is done," Mrs. Mercer said. "What about my—about Mr. Brown's car?"

"It's being towed into town so that our men can go over it."

We were all on our feet, waiting for the next move. Sonia's color had come back, her eyes were shining, she was young again. She dived into her handbag to repair her makeup.

Clay looked at me. "I'm going to hold you and MacIntosh for further questioning."

"Sergeant," Charles said explosively, "if you let Mrs. Kenyon and Paxton go free, I can tell you exactly what is going to happen."

"Now, that would be helpful."

"He'll divvy up with her to keep her quiet until after the trial. Then she is going to have a fatal accident. She'll have to. Paxton can't afford to let her live; any time she wanted to, she could send him to the chair for those two murders."

Sonia, powder compact in her hand, stood stockstill, staring at Charles. With the jerky motion of a mechanical doll she turned her head and looked at Paxton. Then she sank back in her chair as though her knees had given way.

"Tough," Charles said. "Very, very tough. From now on you won't have a single moment free of fear, wondering when it's coming, how it's coming. A knife. A bullet. A rope. A hammer. A drowning accident. A car smashup. Poison. Any one of them at any time."

The perspiration stood out on Sonia's face. Her color was awful. "You—you—" She mouthed the words, staring at him.

"But it's your own fault, you know," Charles told her. "You shouldn't have been so greedy. And you shouldn't have planned to take Mary's life as well as her inheritance."

"Mary!" Sonia clutched at my hand. "Mary, you know what we've always been to each other. Only you don't understand what it's like to be in love. And Jack lost everything after our marriage was made public. I had to make it up to him some way."

"With Mary's money," Charles said.

For days the tension must have been building up in her, the mounting panic. Then she had seen the scaffolding come tumbling down, had seen Jack with that knife between his shoulders, had known the whole

plan had failed. On top of that had come the growing
strain of the past hours. And now stark terror.

"It wasn't fair," she screamed. "It wasn't fair. Why
should Paxton get half? Those awful, disgusting old
women hanging on to their youth. After all, Jack did
all the work, didn't he?"

It was so unbelievable an outburst that for a moment we were all stunned. Then Clay had his gun in
his hand. There was a single shot. The gun dropped
and he clutched his wrist. An arm jerked me around.
Paxton was holding me against him, the gun he had
pulled out of his belt moving from side to side.

"One move and she'll have it," he said.

"You can't get away with this," Clay said.

"If I don't, it will be rough on Mary." Paxton
stepped down out of the trailer, dragging me after
him. I stumbled, nearly sprawling on the ground, and
he jerked me against him again, a living shield. We
were walking backward, step by step, the gun pressed
against my side. Then he picked me up, shoved me
into the police car, got in, gunned the motor, and shot
out of the trailer park at a wicked pace.

A bullet whanged against the back of the car. Then
another. Apparently Grant was shooting at the gas
tank. A third shot fell short. Then we were out of
range.

I sat watching Paxton's pleasant profile. Paxton. It
had been Paxton. The steak knife in Jack's back,
"like a beheading knife," he had said. Brown's skull
crushed by the hammer. Paxton.

"But you didn't kill the little dog," I said aloud.

"That," Paxton said cheerfully, "was Kenyon's con-
tribution. He meant the hammer for me, used it to
keep that dog quiet, and then—found me prepared for
him."

The car went around a curve on two wheels, the
tires screaming, Paxton grabbed at the wheel and
eased his foot on the gas, frightened by his own speed.

I began to realize that the police car was weaving dangerously, that he appeared to have little control. I wondered if Charles had been right when he said that Paxton had overdone it in knocking himself out. He might have a slight concussion. There was small comfort in that; if he smashed up the car, I'd go with it.

"If you are dizzy, you had better slow up. Or maybe it's easier for you this way. One smashup and it will be all over."

"They won't get me," he said confidently.

"You aren't exactly invisible in a police car."

"It isn't necessary to go far. Anyhow, it was the only one left that worked. Jack had let the air out of my tires, damn him! Double-crosser from way back. At least after Sonia got her greedy little claws in him. Before that he was as good a partner as you'd want. He would never have dreamed of trying to bump me off. That was Sonia. It was all Sonia. Well, let's see how she likes it now. Maybe she has learned that I don't care to be made a fool of."

Considerably to my relief he had checked that first reckless speed. His eyes were on the road, his hands firm on the wheel, but I saw that his eyes were narrowed, he was almost squinting. I wondered whether he was having any difficulty with his vision. If he was slightly concussed, it was possible. I had groped for the door handle but I didn't dare turn it. Even at a moderate forty I could kill myself or break a leg. Anyhow, he'd have no difficulty in finding me. There was literally no place to go off the road. No place at all.

The headlights tore holes in the darkness, brushed past clumps of palmetto, past mangrove swamp, past dark gleaming water. The wheels bumped slightly as he ran over some small woods animal.

Terror rode in the car with me. Incongruously, it was filled for a moment with the sweet scent of orange blossoms as we passed a grove of fruit trees.

Then, again, there was nothing but swamp, patches of the high grass of the Everglades, a thickening of interlacing vines in the jungle.

"I might have known Sonia wouldn't play it straight," Paxton said in a virtuous tone that would have made me laugh if I hadn't been so terrified. "After that double cross with the necklace I expected some kind of trick. I came to the trailer park early this morning—yesterday morning—cased the place, staked out in that empty trailer. Then you showed up. At first I thought you were Sonia. Then I heard Mrs. Thomson call you Miss Quarles and give you that bottle of bourbon from Kenyon. That's when I knew you were set up for something. You and me both."

It had been some time since I had heard the tide washing in. Paxton turned onto a narrow dirt road that seemed to lead straight into the jungle. The headlights reflected on mangrove, on tangled vines, on black water, on long grass. We seemed to be going straight into the Everglades.

There was no walking back from that place, Mrs. Mercer had said. *No walking back.*

Paxton was driving almost at a crawl now, easing the car over the rough road. I strained my ears. There must be someone following us. Someone. Grant was armed and Clay hadn't been completely incapacitated. And there was Charles. Charles would come, unless my lack of faith had disgusted him completely

Abruptly, Paxton brought the car to a halt. "We're getting out here."

It was bad enough in the car. On foot it would be worse. On foot it would be fatal. I didn't budge.

The gun was in his hand again. "Out!"

"That s Brown's gun, isn t it?"

"Yes."

"Why did you kill him?"

"What else could I do?" he said in the tone of

a much-injured man. "You think I like killing people? I knew the score when I heard him talking to you. I knew he was loaded with enough to buy the necklace. Up to then, I hadn't even been told that Kenyon had changed his fence. That was probably little Sonia's doing. And at that she'll probably come out clean as a whistle because she looks so pretty and helpless. Women!"

For a moment his head dropped a trifle and he rubbed his eyes with his free hand. I hoped he was badly concussed, though I wasn't sure whether that would help me or not.

Unexpectedly he laughed. "Say, that was quite a beating Brown gave you."

"You enjoyed it, didn't you?"

"Right up to the hilt. Every moment. Then, when he slipped and you got away, I went in. He turned over the cash and took the necklace without a fuss or a complaint. He was scared stiff of murder, didn't want any part of it. All he wanted was out. But I couldn't let him go, of course. Once he got away from me, he was bound to report Jack's murder. Mrs. Mercer would inform the police that he had gone to the Scotty so he'd have to admit knowing about the murder.

"He got away from me as fast as he could and headed for his car. I waited until he got in, smashed him over the head with the hammer Jack had used on the dog and intended for me. He'd dropped it in the Scotty when he died and I took it away. Kind of poetic justice in that, wasn't there?"

"You'd think so, of course. I don't understand people like you. Is there something wrong with your brains or are you just vain? Who was it who analyzed the essentially silly mind of a criminal who can't reason? You hear of cases: a man who has spent fifteen of his thirty-five years in prison and still thinks he is smart, that he can get away with it next time."

That was a mistake. All I wanted was to postpone as long as possible the moment when I would have to step out of the car into jungle.

The gun nudged me. "Out!"

There was nothing left of me but a quivering jelly of fear, not even any basic courage or human dignity. I whimpered, "Don't leave me here. Not in the jungle."

Paxton leaned over me, his cheek brushing against mine. I shrank back, assailed by a new terror.

"Please! Please!"

He began to laugh. "Take it easy. You're safe with me."

"Safe?" I repeated unbelievingly.

"You won't have to make the supreme sacrifice. You are safe from a fate worse than death. Women don't interest me. That's why I had to set up a partnership with Kenyon. He didn't mind much, even with the old ones."

"A fate worse than death. But death?"

He made no reply and I clawed at his hand, trying to prevent him from opening the door.

"It's up to you," he said. "I shoot you now or you get out without being shot and take your chance. I don't want to shoot you. Not on your account. Frankly, I don't give a damn. But sound carries."

He jerked my hands away, opened the door and pushed me out onto a tangle of mangrove roots.

"What do you have to gain?" I said desperately.

"Time. Give me two hours and no one would ever find me. Stand back."

I moved cautiously to one side. The road had come to an end. On three sides there was nothing but jungle and black gleaming water. The Everglades. The only firm ground was the road along which we had come.

Paxton got out, leaned inside, released the brake, gunned the motor, and leaped out of the way as the car moved forward slowly and slid down into the water. When the waves had stopped lapping the ground, he took my arm and pushed me ahead. Then he switched on the flashlight he had taken from the police car and I saw the rowboat with the outboard motor.

"I came across this when I was scouting around yesterday morning. You'll find some sort of boat on nearly all these canals. The way most Indians supplement their diet. Good fishing in there. Now get in."

"No! No, I won't."

He shrugged, and lifted the gun. With a sob, I got into the boat and he followed me, felt for the oars, and began to row. "I can't use the outboard motor because sound travels too far."

There was no sound at all but the faint splash of the oars striking the water, a creaking of oarlocks, a dry rustle of vines as a light breeze rose. Then, even through the darkness I began to see the gleam of water. Dawn was breaking. Even through the thickness of the jungle, I was aware of that. Ahead I could see a hammock, one of those tiny islands that appear here and there in the Everglades. I gathered myself together. If I could reach the gun, if I could jump—

"You're rocking the boat," Paxton said mildly. "I don't advise it. Take a look down there. Moccasins. Alligators. Maybe even crocs."

The boat grated against a clump of mangrove. Paxton reached out to hang onto a thick branch, steadying the boat.

"This is where you get out." He laughed. "Last stop, Mary."

17

There was hardly more than enough clear space on which to stand. I held on to a thick branch of mangrove, listening. The sound of the rowboat had died away but I was still too frightened to scream, afraid that Paxton would return and shoot me.

Little by little, the sky grew bright and the jungle awakened. Around me unseen things were stirring, coming to life. A huge blue heron rose from almost beside me, startling me almost to death. From where I stood there was nothing but Everglades, stretching forever. In one of the motels there had been a little tourist's book about the Everglades, four thousand square miles of them. How could anyone find me here?

A light breeze set the grass to rustling. I found myself pivoting, my eyes searching wildly for the sources of those sounds. By daylight the water looked more menacing than it had by the headlights of the car. A fish leaped and fell back with a splash, scaring me, so that I almost lost my balance and followed it, and I snatched wildly at thick, heavy grasses. They held me but the toothlike edges cut my fingers nearly to the bone. I remembered reading the attractive statement that they could cut a man's body to ribbons. This was a world where nature hated man, fighting him with all her resources.

Beside my hand something moved and I saw the huge coiled moccasin on a branch beside me and sprang back, sobbing with terror. This was the stuff of nightmares. I wished now, wished with all my heart, that Paxton had shot me. Anything was better than this creeping horror, waiting for death from slimy things, crawling things, the last indignity.

Near my foot what I took for a piece of rope writhed almost over my shoe, struck and I heard a squeal. The snake had caught some tiny rodent. Nature red in tooth and claw. If anyone ever again dared to speak to me of benevolent Mother Nature, I'd—but I remembered that no one was likely to speak to me again of anything.

A log floated on the dark water and then I saw the small red eyes. An alligator. *No walking back.*

Slowly the sun began to rise and the heat to settle. I found myself slapping at mosquitoes. Charles's clothes, which had seemed so warm and comfortable during the night, were like a blanket under which I sweltered, and my sunburn burned like fire.

Overhead there was a faint movement, and I looked up with the wild hope that a helicopter was hunting for me, though there was no reason why anyone would assume I was in the Glades. Then I saw the wood ibises; there must have been a dozen, exquisite in flight against the dark jungle. They were so beautiful that for a moment I forgot even my disappointment, caught up in sheer, heart-stopping loveliness.

A faint splash jerked my head around toward the dark waterway along which Paxton and I had come. Something was moving. Around the bend I saw the rowboat, then the Indian. I shouted at the top of my voice, the sound sending half a dozen birds whose presence I had not suspected, rising out of the bushes.

"Help!" I called. "Help!" The Indian looked at me and I waved both arms like a madwoman. "Help!"

After a moment he waved back at me and then, with a churning of water, he sent the boat back the way it had come. This was disaster so final, so unexpected, that I could only stare blankly.

Time passed then. I had cried so long that there

were no tears left. Even my terror had become numbed by loss of hope. Yet I stood in the same cleared spot, watching automatically for snakes.

How long I stood there I don't know. I don't seem to have thought of anything. I waited but I was waiting for nothing.

When the new sound broke the quiet, I was barely aware of it at first. Then it grew louder. An outboard motor. I tried to shout but I seemed to have no more voice, only a hoarse croak that could not carry. This had happened in nightmares, too; screaming for help and having no sound come out.

Then someone shouted, "Mary! Mary! Where are you?"

The rowboat with the outboard motor came around the curve. This time the Seminole was handling it while Charles was searching the jungle.

"Mary! There she is!" At Charles's cry, the Seminole steered the boat toward the little hammock and Charles leaped out to gather me in his arms.

II

The next few days have been blotted out. Now and then I remember some of the unspeakable dreams, but they are fading rapidly. After that, I was fully conscious but so apathetic that I had no interest in what went on around me. I grasped that I was in a hospital, that I had double pneumonia, that the height and duration of my fever had set something of a record, that my condition on arrival had caused a sensation.

Now and then I roused to see the curious canopy over me and realize I was in an oxygen tent. Now and then I was aware of people around me. White-clad nurses came and went, eying me with avid curiosity but asking no questions. A surprisingly young-looking doctor issued stern orders to prevent anyone from talking to me.

I saw faces that came and went: Charles, Sergeant Clay, Charles, Mrs. Miller, Charles, Mrs. Bateson, Charles. Charles. There was only one person who did not come, did not send any message, but I didn't ask. I was afraid to ask about Sonia.

Then one morning when Mrs. Miller came I was sitting up in bed, eating a huge breakfast and demanding my clothes.

She was one broad smile. "Well," she said in delight, "you look like yourself now. You had us pretty worried for a while."

"How long have I been here?"

"Nearly ten days."

"And you've been here all the time?"

She laughed. "Mrs. Thomson has practically taken us over. Bakes homemade bread. Found a dog for Sam to play with. She even offered to baby-sit."

"You mean you're still staying at the trailer park?"

"Did you think," she asked indignantly, "after what you did for Sam we'd leave until you were out of danger?" Her face was suffused with laughter. "Mrs. Thomson said she'd like to come and see you, do something real nice for you, but maybe you wouldn't like to see her."

"How right she is!" Then I laughed too. "What caused this change of heart?"

"The police have been digging into her past life and she's very unhappy about it. Practically a reformed character. But, my dear," and she went off into a gale of laughter, "can you imagine? She's trying to find if there's any way she can sue Paxton for starting the fire in the trailer park."

The young-looking doctor came in, and she broke off abruptly. "Sorry, Doctor, I was just telling her—"

"Give her another day before you exchange girlish confidences."

"Another day! Nothing of the kind," I said firmly. "I want some clothes. I want to get up. I want to know what's been happening."

He looked at my chart and grinned. "Give her her clothes. She can sit up for half an hour if she behaves herself."

"Oh, I forgot. I haven't any clothes."

"I got you some yesterday," Mrs. Miller said. "A small and inadequate thank-you for what you did for Sam. Wait a minute."

When she had gone I turned to the doctor. "It would be easier to know, honestly it would. I'll go crazy wondering and worrying. Anything is better than uncertainty."

"Let's not lose all we've gained. Let's see how you feel after you've got dressed up."

I felt wonderful. With Mrs. Miller's help I put on a thin yellow dress, though she had to do most of the work. My legs felt like cooked macaroni when I tried to stand up. The sunburn had gone and most of the bruises. Except for one deep scratch on my cheek, some cuts on my fingers from the saw grass, and the gash on my shin where Brown had kicked me, I was as good as new. At least I would be when I got back some stiffening in my legs and regained some of the weight I had lost.

Mrs. Miller brushed my hair and arranged it for me. She had even remembered makeup. By the time we got through, we were both delighted. I'd never have that special quality that made Sonia so irresistible, just as I didn't have her wonderful eyes and vivid smile, but I looked a lot different from the beatnik I had been.

"That's the way you looked the first time I saw you," Mrs. Miller said. "I remember thinking at the time that competition was going to be rugged. But here in the hospital, what with those bruises—my dear, there was one day when you were at least six different colors—and that fever going on and on, there were some moments when I wondered whether you would pull through. I've been dying to know what happened to you. According to the papers you were kidnaped and then left to die in the Everglades."

Before I could answer, the doctor came back. Mrs. Miller had settled me in a big chair, with a cushion under me and another one at my back. I felt exhausted but exhilarated and triumphant.

"You've been overdoing it." Then he gave me an infectious boyish grin. "But, by the lord Harry, it was worth it! You don't look much like that dismal, battered creature they brought in here ten days ago. Okay, I guess you can get some answers to your questions now. But only half an hour. And I warn you, we'll hold a stopwatch on him."

At his nod Mrs. Miller went out with him. To my disappointment it was Sergeant Clay who came in, looking very spruced up in his uniform, his arm in a sling.

For a moment he stood looking down at me, a queer expression on his face, and then he whistled. "And I thought—" He shook his head. "No wonder you've got a hard-boiled guy like MacIntosh running around in circles."

I could feel color flooding my cheeks and I said tartly, "I suppose he's doing his running in a cell."

Clay laughed and pulled a chair toward him rather awkwardly, and sat down. "He's spent most of his time hanging around the hospital, driving the doctors and nurses crazy."

"Oh. How's your arm?"

"Not too bad. He got me through the wrist. They'll have me using it again before long, though I won't be much good at target practice for a while."

It seemed odd that we should be on such relaxed and friendly terms, considering that my last sight of him had been when he was about to arrest me for murder.

"Well, what do you want to know?"

"Everything," I said simply.

"That's quite an order but I'll see what I can do."
He added soberly, "I guess you've got that much
coming to you. I gave you a hard time. We don't get
much serious crime around here and I was out of my
depth. I didn't quite know how to handle it. You've
got to admit that, walking in cold on two dead bodies,
a stolen diamond necklace, a gal who had been beaten
up, MacIntosh and Paxton claiming to have been
knocked out, it was a mess.

"But I can tell you this much, Miss Quarles, after a
while you were the only one I had completely elimi-
nated in my mind. At first, looking the way you did
and that cockeyed story, well—" He grinned ruefully.
"But with everything piling up on you, you were hell-
bent on clearing everyone else. According to you, the
Millers were out of it; the Browns were out of it; Mrs.
Kenyon was out of it. You were breaking your neck
to clear them all. And you were burned up when I let
Mrs. Kenyon see her husband's body without warning
her first; you were fighting mad because no one had
looked after the Seminole's hands."

"Then why did you let me, let everyone, think you
believed I was guilty?"

"I thought it would cause a reaction," he admitted
shamelessly, "to kind of prod all of you. Get you
talking. Even a good liar trips up when he talks too
much. And Mrs. Kenyon isn't a good liar, just a congenital liar. Which isn't the same thing."

He looked at me uneasily. "I suppose you'd like to
have me fired for letting Paxton grab you like that.
We should have searched him but he looked so
knocked out I didn't think it was necessary. It was
Brown's gun he had. Slipped it inside his belt. That's
why he kept that jacket so neatly buttoned. Brown, by
the way, was a guy named Warburton, a fence the
Canadian authorities have been looking for, for a long
time. They didn't express any deep grief about his
passing.

"Well, as you know, Paxton hauled you into the police car before we could move. Grant had his gun out but he was afraid to use it in case he got you instead. There wasn't a single car that would run. MacIntosh started off on foot, running after you like someone at an Olympic track meet. And I'll bet he broke some records. Then the Seminole shot past us on his bicycle. That work you put in on his hands seems to have made an impression, and he'd been taking in the whole business. Didn't think much of Mrs. Kenyon."

He saw my expression, coughed, and went on rather hastily. "Well, the Indian caught up with MacIntosh who sent him on to town to get help while he kept prowling along the main road and all the little side roads. The Seminole got to town, reported, and things went into action; barricades were put up; every man on the force, state police, and all the deputy sheriffs were notified."

"But Paxton had plenty of time to reach town before the Indian could get there on a bicycle! Oh, I forgot, he sank the police car."

"Yes. Well, time passed and the police car hadn't come through, so we figured he had abandoned it. By that time, it was pretty clear that he had taken you into the Everglades. I don't think there was a single human being, with the exception of MacIntosh, who didn't take for granted that he had killed you. But that stubborn Scot wouldn't give up. He and the Seminole pooled resources and began to follow every side road. It wasn't until nearly noon that they found the place where the police car had gone into the water. It was completely submerged. MacIntosh was frantic. Finally he dived down to make sure you weren't inside. And that, Miss Quarles, is something I wouldn't have done. Not in that water.

"Then an Indian in a rowboat came along, shouting that there was a crazy woman in the Glades, yelling her head off, so MacIntosh and the Seminole took his boat and went in after you. You must have had quite a time."

I didn't answer that. The best thing to do with nightmares is to try to blot them out completely.

"Did Paxton get away?"

Clay began to laugh. "He did not. And that was the damnedest thing! Would you have guessed the guy is totally bald? Some childhood skin infection or something. Well, he pulled off his wig and put on a thin, reddish mustache and thick-lensed glasses, stripped down to shorts and sport shirt, and when I saw him I would never have recognized him if it hadn't been for that black eye he'd given himself. He even walked differently. He came out of that side road after getting rid of you and the car, and he was hightailing it along when a car came up behind him. Not many people walking at dawn, miles from anywhere.

"He hailed the car and asked for a lift. Said he'd been walking on doctor's orders, but he'd overdone it. Looked like it, too. Kind of dizzy and he had trouble focusing." Clay leaned back in his chair and roared with laughter.

"What's so funny?"

"Well, he'd hit himself so hard he had concussion. He wasn't seeing too well and he hadn't noticed the sign on the car, DEPUTY SHERIFF.

"The driver picked him up, pumped him casually about where he was staying, and Paxton got uneasy. Pointed out the next house along the road. Said he was visiting friends there. Only thing was, it turned out to be the deputy's own house. So Paxton finished his trip to town in handcuffs and he is now in jail, charged with first-degree murder."

I shivered. Then I said, "Were you very much surprised?"

"When he pulled out that gun, I sure was. But of course I'd known he was lying from the start."

"How?"

"Well, that story about sleeping out because he was so broke. Did you take a gander at those slacks with the knife-edge crease? And that jacket without a wrinkle in it? He hadn't been sleeping out in those clothes but he was trying to improvise, to talk himself out of a nasty spot."

"You think he did knock himself out?"

"Yes. The Seminole showed us the tree under which he found him and sure enough there were signs on the trunk where he had skinned his face. He ran into a lot of bad luck but the worst was when he accidentally dropped a match in that pool of gasoline and started the fire. He had no way to escape; there was nothing left for him to do but try to bluff it out."

"But the money and the necklace?"

"He'd hidden them in the Seminole's shack when the fire engine came. We found the stuff stuck away in an empty coffee tin."

"Can you prove anything, except that he took me away with him?"

"Well, he was most ill-advised," Clay said, smiling broadly, "when he stripped the bodies, you see. He had all Brown's papers, the money you lent Kenyon and your car keys, neatly put away with the necklace and Brown's wad. Ever see thirty-eight thousand dollars in cold cash? It's a beautiful sight, lady. A beautiful sight."

He laughed. "Yes, we've been doing right well on our own, and we've also had some rather insistent help from your admirers."

"Admirers?"

"Don't pretend you don't know about MacIntosh. And there's a fellow named Richard Burgess—"

"Richard!"

"He got here a week ago, breathing fire and threats. He had a man from the New York police force with him, bringing along a bartender who admitted he had doped you and given the story to a local scandal-monger. Got paid five hundred dollars for it. The letter of instructions had been typed on the machine at the hotel where the Kenyons were staying. By the time Burgess got through with me, I felt as though I had been skinned, inch by inch, with a dull knife. He seems to think a lot of you."

"He's an old friend," I said rather inadequately, knowing perfectly well that Clay remembered what Charles had said about my planning to marry Richard.

"So I gathered. He prepared a statement for me to sign." Clay's grin was rather forced. "Made a damned fool of me but I guess I owed it to you."

"What on earth did he want with a statement?"

"He sent it to some radio broadcaster in your home town. And he sent it off with a blistering letter that ended by saying that if this statement was not read, word by word, as it had been written, the Town Crier would find himself out of a job if Burgess personally had to buy the damned radio station."

"Well," I said weakly, "what got into him?"

"I'll let him tell you himself."

The door opened and the young doctor came in. "All right. Time's up." He nodded to the nurse who came to take my arm and help me to my feet. "That's all for today."

Clay went out and I settled back on my pillows. After being so impatient to get up, it was good to lie flat again. It occurred to me belatedly that Clay hadn't, after all, told me what I wanted to know.

18

The next day I held court in the hospital. Mrs. Miller came back and again helped me to dress. She had brought Mrs. Bateson to see me and the latter was waiting on the sundeck.

When I was dressed, a nurse pushed my wheel chair—though I was really able to walk—onto the deck where there seemed to be a number of people. It was not until the young doctor came charging into their midst and drove them away that I realized they were reporters and photographers. It hadn't occurred to me that Sonia's involvement in the murders was bound to attract newsmen from all over the country. A few days later I saw the Sunday feature story with pictures of Sonia and me, side by side. I pushed them aside and never read the story.

When the doctor had routed out the reporters, with strict orders that I was not to be interviewed until after I was discharged from the hospital—"this girl has had a close brush with death; she needs to build up her strength"—there was no one left but Mrs. Miller and Mrs. Bateson. The latter came beaming to take my hand and pat it.

Bateson, she said happily, had been released a few days earlier and he was doing fine, just taking life easy and lying around in the sun. Enjoying it, too. Some new people had come to the park and there were a few men of his own age who were going to teach him to play shuffleboard, so things were picking up, what with a bingo night and all.

She got to her feet. "Well, I've got to get back to Bateson. Mrs. Miller is driving me. Everyone has been real friendly." Her eyes twinkled. "Except for Mr. Mercer."

"Mr. Mercer!"

"He came down here and what all he didn't say to that silly wife of his was a caution. Never saw anyone so blazing mad in all my life. She was right subdued."

When the two women had gone, I moved over to a deck chair and stretched out, looking over the little town, over the blue ocean with its soaring gulls and awkward pelicans, over the palm trees and hibiscus hedges, over the bridges with their lines of patient fishermen. Such a quiet, sleepy town. When I turned my head I could see the jungle and, even with the sun pouring down on me, I shivered.

A nurse brought me lunch on a tray, propped pillows behind me, urged me to eat, an unnecessary request because I was eating like a stevedore.

"When I think of what you looked like when you were brought in here," she said, "I can't believe it. I undressed you. I never saw anyone more marked up in my life. And what wasn't bruises and cuts and gashes and sunburn was mosquito bites. And your face swollen out of shape. I never would have guessed then that you were a beauty."

"Me?" I said with more amazement than grammar.

"Beautiful but so god-awful dumb," Richard said, and came across the sundeck, looking more like an eagle than ever. With a beaming smile for both of us, the nurse went away.

"I seem to have caused you and everyone an awful lot of trouble," I said, recalling how he hated to travel. "I owe you such an awful lot."

"For God's sake," he snapped, "don't start feeling apologetic. You're the one who rates a little consideration and I'm going to see that you get it. You were set up to take a murder rap, you were nearly killed, you were beaten to a pulp, you were kidnaped. What are you apologizing for?" He glared at me.

I laughed. "In my weakened state I shouldn't be bullied."

"Don't give me that. You're blooming."

I braced myself. "Tell me about Sonia. No one has told me about her. I have to know, Richard."

"She's denying everything right now, of course, but apparently she gave away the whole thing at the trailer park. Every claim she has made has been proved to be false. Especially that elaborate business of setting you up as a drinker at the trailer park. She's been caught flat-footed about it being you. And that's no credit to you, Mary. Of all the tomfool things to do, sleeping out on the beach!"

"What is it now?" I asked in resignation.

"A stroke of luck you don't deserve. Some amateur photographer got pictures of you asleep on the beach. Took them to a newspaper and the editor thought they were pictures of Sonia Colette, published them, and presented you with a clean bill of health."

"And Sergeant Clay was so sure I was lying about that."

"Actually," Richard said, "he was confused in the beginning but he was tipped off to Sonia almost at once. He said one of the first things she did was to pull a kind of striptease on him, with her skirt hiked up nearly to her hip. So he naturally wondered why this attempt to misdirect his attention."

"What is going to happen to her? She didn't kill either man. They can't—do anything very bad to her, can they?"

"Well, a lot of the story is out in the open now, Mary. The police know Sonia was perfectly aware of that singularly ugly partnership between her husband and Paxton. They know she set a pretty little trap for you. They found that flask of Kenyon's loaded with dope of some kind, which corroborates what Gus told them about the incident in Lloydsville. All that is hard to account for unless you were to be involved in Paxton's murder."

"Will Paxton accuse her?"

"He can't. All he can do is sit tight and keep his mouth shut and deny everything. But the police have all they need to make a first-degree charge stick. Then your friend MacIntosh"—for a moment his eyes rested on my face—"raised hell with his client. She has just informed him that as her husband has died of a heart attack, she is no longer afraid to testify. She'll pin everything she can on Kenyon, largely in hope that she can involve Sonia."

Richard lighted his pipe, taking his time. "Sonia is in for a bad time. But you can never tell with a male jury. She is beautiful, and once she has learned her lines she can put them over. She has a good lawyer. She might just pull a fast one. Unless you—"

"No," I said.

He looked at his watch, got up quickly. "Take care of yourself."

"Must you go? I'm not at all tired."

"I have a plane to catch. Going home this afternoon. I'll be back when I'm needed." He put his hand on my shoulder. When he smiled, there was all the warmth and kindness of the past in his face. "I'm leaving you in good hands. But come back to Lloydsville some time. They'll kill the fatted calf." His hand tightened on my shoulder but he did not attempt to kiss me again.

And then Charles came, Charles in a sport shirt open at the throat and wearing white slacks. He pulled up a straight chair beside me. For a long time he did not speak at all, he just looked at me. For some reason there seemed to be nothing that had to be said.

"Doctor tells me you'll be leaving here tomorrow." He reached out to take my hand, to turn it over and study the lines.

"Fortunetelling?" I asked.

He bent over and kissed the palm of my hand lightly. "I'm going to have my work cut out, looking after you. I'm thinking vaguely of getting a dog collar and a leash when we are married."

"We're going to be married?"

"Why, yes, didn't you know?" he asked in surprise. "On March fifteenth. Clay knows, your friend Burgess knows—and that's a fine guy, Mary—and I was sort of under the impression that I had mentioned it to you."

"Well, of course, you've had a lot on your mind," I said reasonably. "You couldn't be expected to remember a trifle like that."

"My God, are you going to be one of those understanding wives?"

I laughed. "If you think that you are living in a fool's paradise."

"It's a nice place to be." He drew me up to my feet and stood holding me lightly. "Room for you, too. When you are well enough—"

"I'm well enough now," I said, and walked into his arms. As he had said, it was a nice place to be.

Foreboding mansions,
moonlight and the moaning wind
... a setting for romance,
intrigue and the supernatural

GOTHIC MYSTERIES

DELL BOOKS

**If you cannot obtain copies of these titles from your local bookseller, just
send the price (plus 15c per copy for handling and postage) to Dell Books,
Post Office Box 1000, Pinebrook, N. J. 07058. No postage or handling charge
is required on any order of five or more books.**